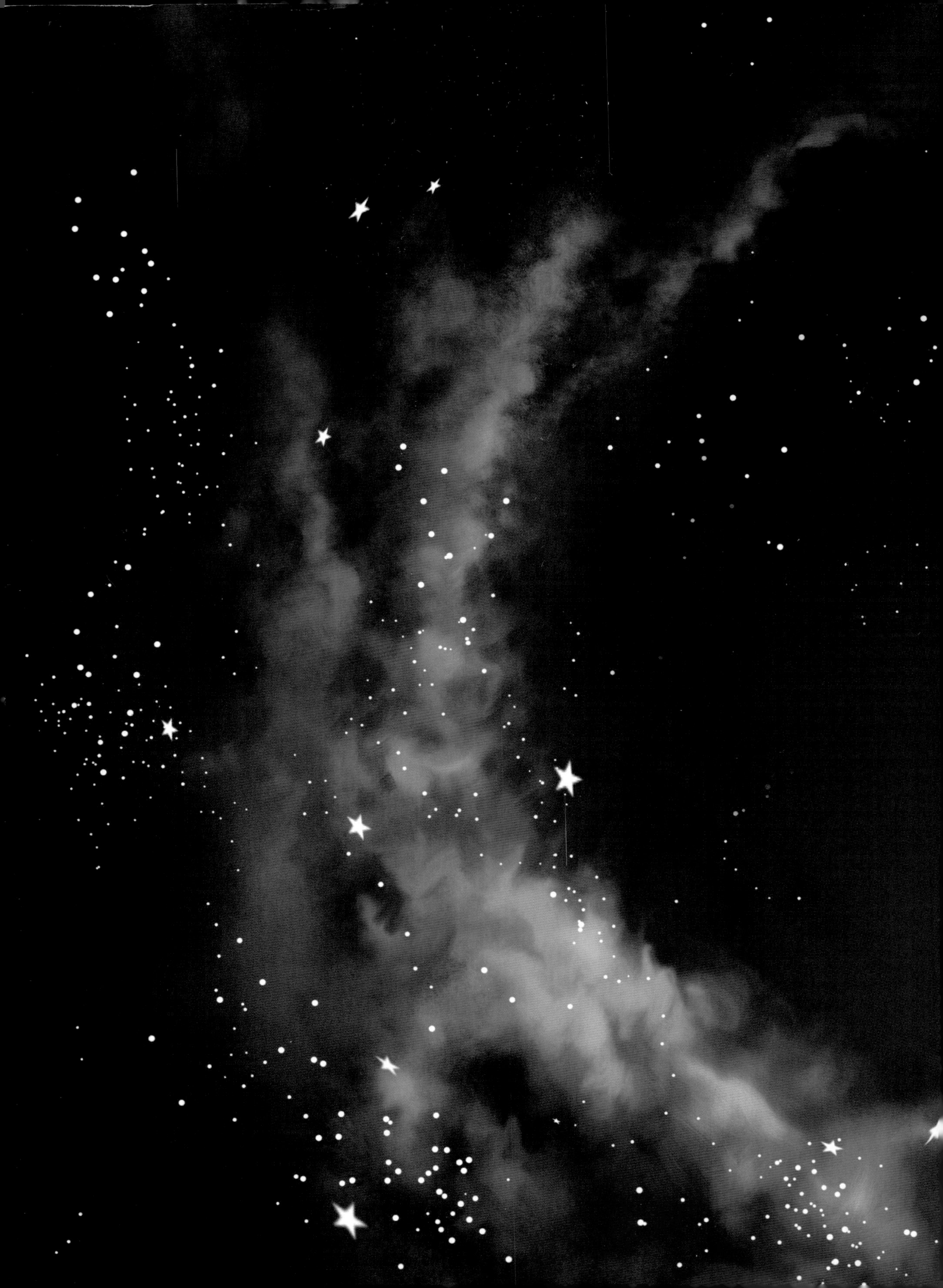

My dear Rose,

It is time once again to embark on a new adventure, now that our journey across the clocks and cogs of the Planet of Time is over and we have found the Great Timekeeper.

During our stay, Fox and I learned that we should not try to do everything ourselves but rather take each day as it comes and seek help when we need it, even from the most unexpected sources. There is no time like the present to make progress toward our goals, and by working together, we can achieve our dreams in the fullness of time.

The Little Prince

First American edition published in 2014 by Graphic Universe™.

Le Petit Prince®

based on the masterpiece by Antoine de Saint-Exupéry

© 2014 LPPM
An animated series based on the novel *Le Petit Prince* by Antoine de Saint-Exupéry
Developed for television by Matthieu Delaporte, Alexandre de la Patellière, and Bertrand Gatignol
Directed by Pierre-Alain Chartier

© 2014 ÉDITIONS GLÉNAT
Copyright © 2014 by Lerner Publishing Group, Inc., for the current edition

Graphic Universe™ is a trademark of Lerner Publishing Group, Inc.

Graphic Universe™
A division of Lerner Publishing Group, Inc.
241 First Avenue North
Minneapolis, MN 55401 USA

For reading levels and more information, look up this title at www.lernerbooks.com.

Library of Congress Cataloging-in-Publication Data
Bruneau, Clotilde.
   [Planète des Cublix. English]
   The planet of the Cublix / story by Maud Loisillier and Diane Morel ; design and illustrations by Elyum Studio ; adaptation by Clotilde Bruneau ; translation, Anne Collins Smith and Owen Smith. — First American edition.
       pages   cm. — (The little prince ; #19)
   ISBN 978-0-7613-8769-5 (lib. bdg. : alk. paper)
   ISBN 978-1-4677-4665-6 (eBook)
   1. Graphic novels. I. Loisillier, Maud. II. Morel, Diane. III. Smith, Anne Collins, translator. IV. Smith, Owen (Owen M.), translator. V. Saint-Exupéry, Antoine de, 1900-1944. Petit Prince. VI. Elyum Studio. VII. Petit Prince (Television program) VIII. Title.
   PZ7.7.B8Pk 2014
   741.5`944—dc23   2014000750

Manufactured in the United States of America
1 — DP — 7/15/14

THE NEW ADVENTURES
BASED ON THE MASTERPIECE BY ANTOINE DE SAINT-EXUPÉRY

The Little Prince

THE PLANET OF THE CUBLIX

Based on the animated series and an original story by Maud Loisillier and Diane Morel

Story: Clotilde Bruneau
Art: Diane Fayolle
Backgrounds: Jérôme Benoît
Coloring: Moonsun
Editing: Christine Chatal
Editorial Consultant: Didier Convard

Translation: Anne and Owen Smith

Graphic Universe™ • Minneapolis

THE LITTLE PRINCE

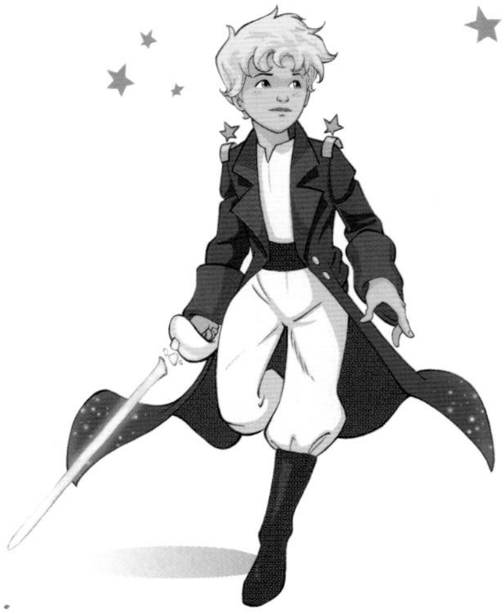

The Little Prince has extraordinary gifts. His sense of wonder allows him to discover what no one else can see. The Little Prince can communicate with all the beings in the universe, even the animals and plants. His powers grow over the course of his adventures.

The Prince's uniform:
When he transforms into the uniform of a prince, he is more agile and quick. When faced with difficult situations, the Little Prince also uses a sword that lets him sketch and bring to life anything from his imagination.

His sketchbook:
When he is not in his Prince's clothing, the Little Prince carries a sketchbook. When he blows on the pages, they take wing and form objects that he'll find very useful. Like his sword, it's powered by stardust collected on his travels.

FOX

A grouch, a trickster, and, so he says, interested only in his next meal, Fox is in reality the Little Prince's best friend. As such, he is always there to give him help but also just as much to help him to grow and to learn about the world.

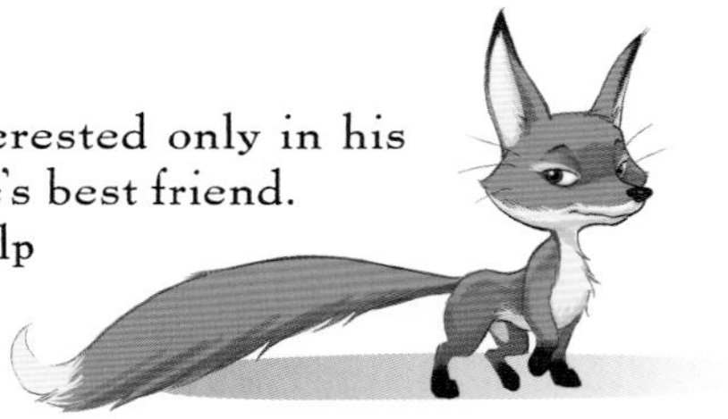

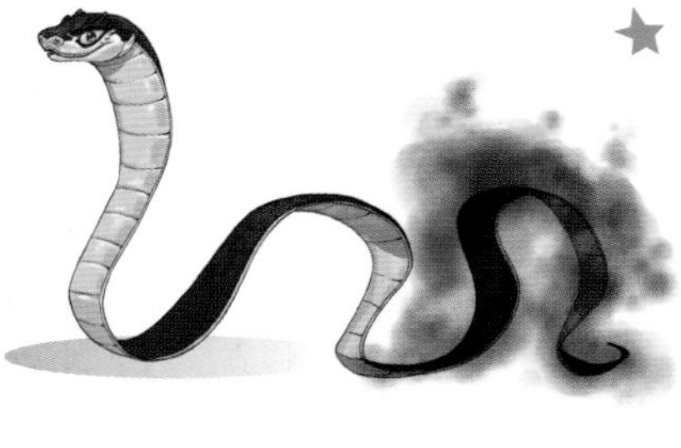

THE SNAKE

Even though the Little Prince still does not know exactly why, there can be no doubt that the Snake has set his mind to plunging the entire universe into darkness! And to accomplish his goal, this malicious being is ready to use any form of deception. However, the Snake never takes action himself. He prefers to bring out the wickedness in those beings he has chosen to bite, tempting them to put their own worlds in danger.

THE GLOOMIES

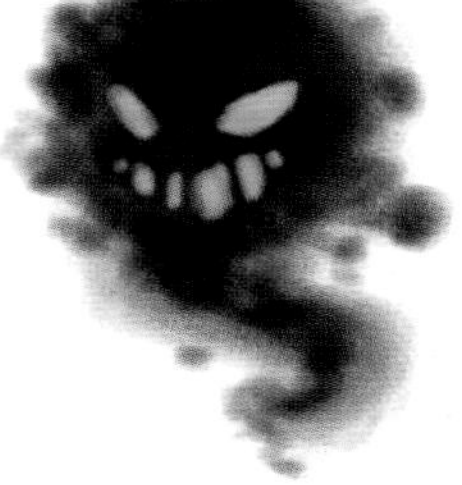

When people who have been "bitten" by the Snake have completely destroyed their own planets, they become Gloomies, slaves to their Snake master. The Gloomies act as a group and carry out the Snake's most vile orders so he can get the better of the Little Prince!

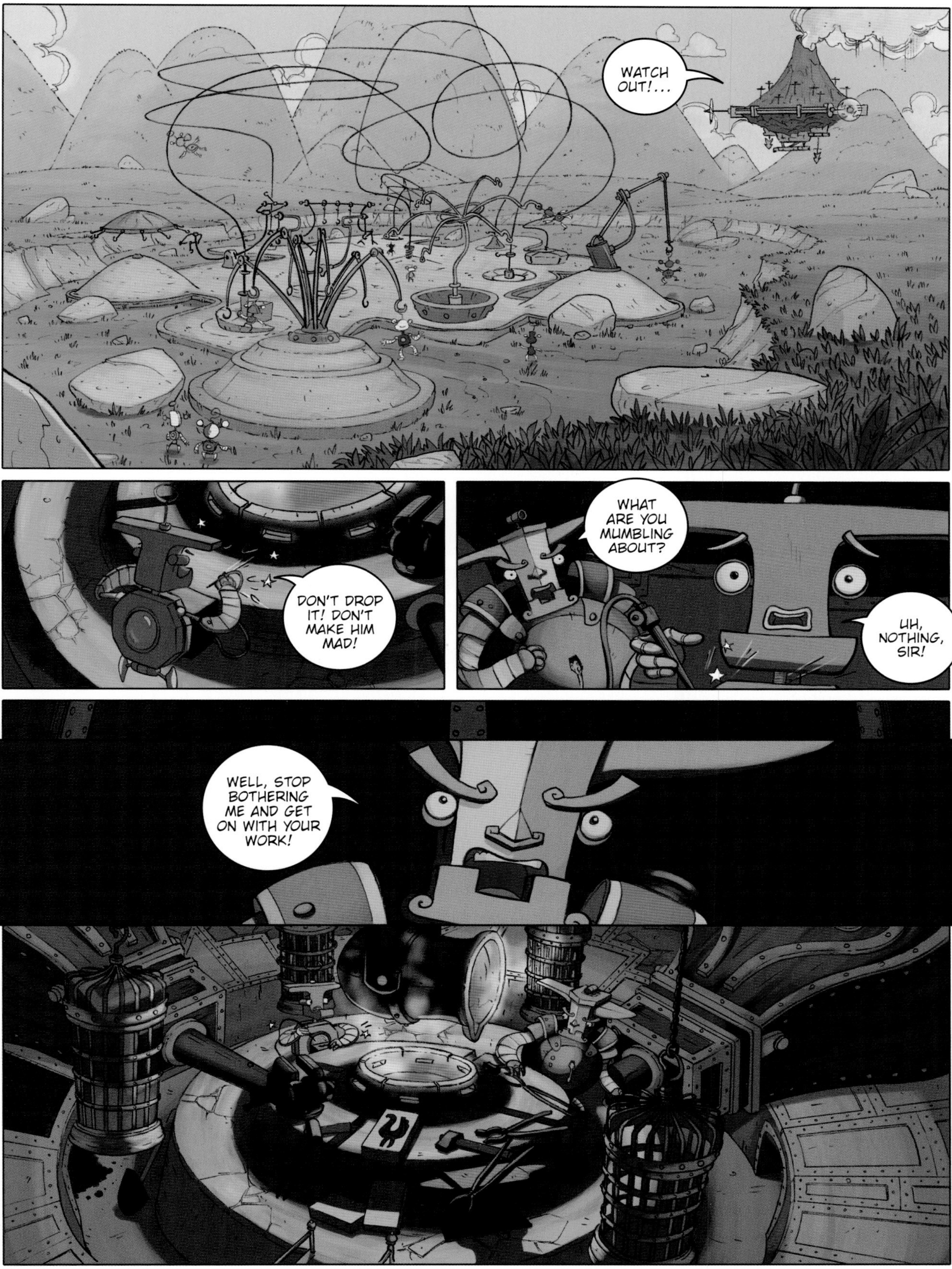
WATCH OUT!...
DON'T DROP IT! DON'T MAKE HIM MAD!
WHAT ARE YOU MUMBLING ABOUT?
UH, NOTHING, SIR!
WELL, STOP BOTHERING ME AND GET ON WITH YOUR WORK!

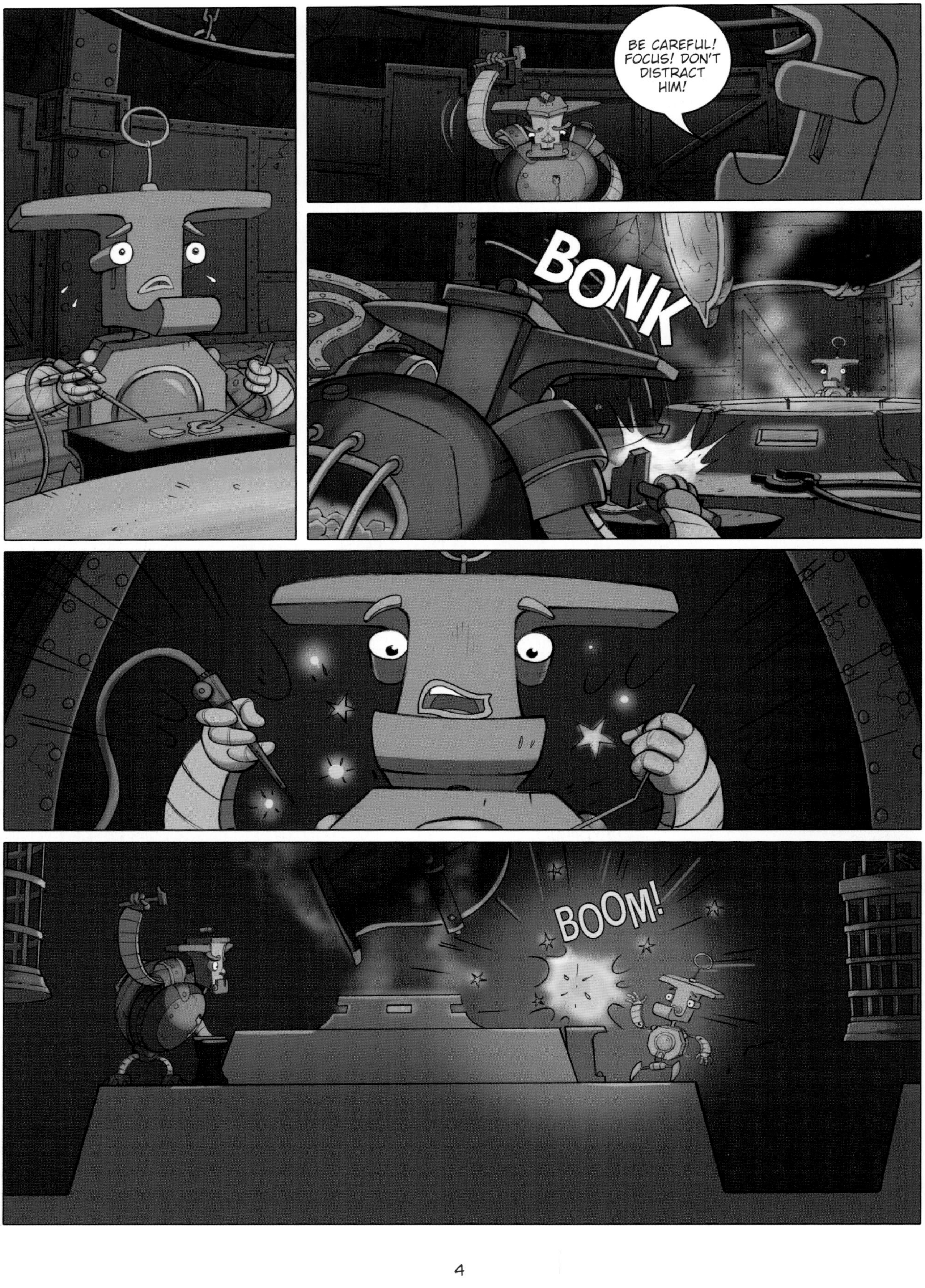
BE CAREFUL! FOCUS! DON'T DISTRACT HIM!
BONK
BOOM!

ALUMNIIIIX!

WHAT AM I GOING TO DO WITH YOU? YOU CAN'T EVEN MAKE A SIMPLE REPAIR!

I...I'M SORRY!

IT'S BAD ENOUGH YOU CAN ONLY REPAIR WHIRLIGIGS! IF YOU CAN'T EVEN DO THAT RIGHT, YOU'RE COMPLETELY USELESS TO ME!

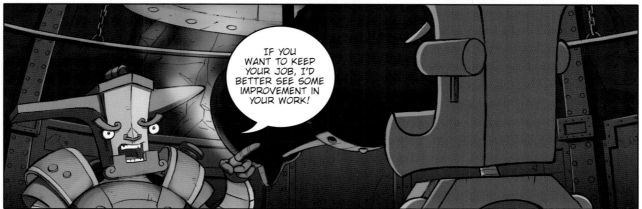

IF YOU WANT TO KEEP YOUR JOB, I'D BETTER SEE SOME IMPROVEMENT IN YOUR WORK!

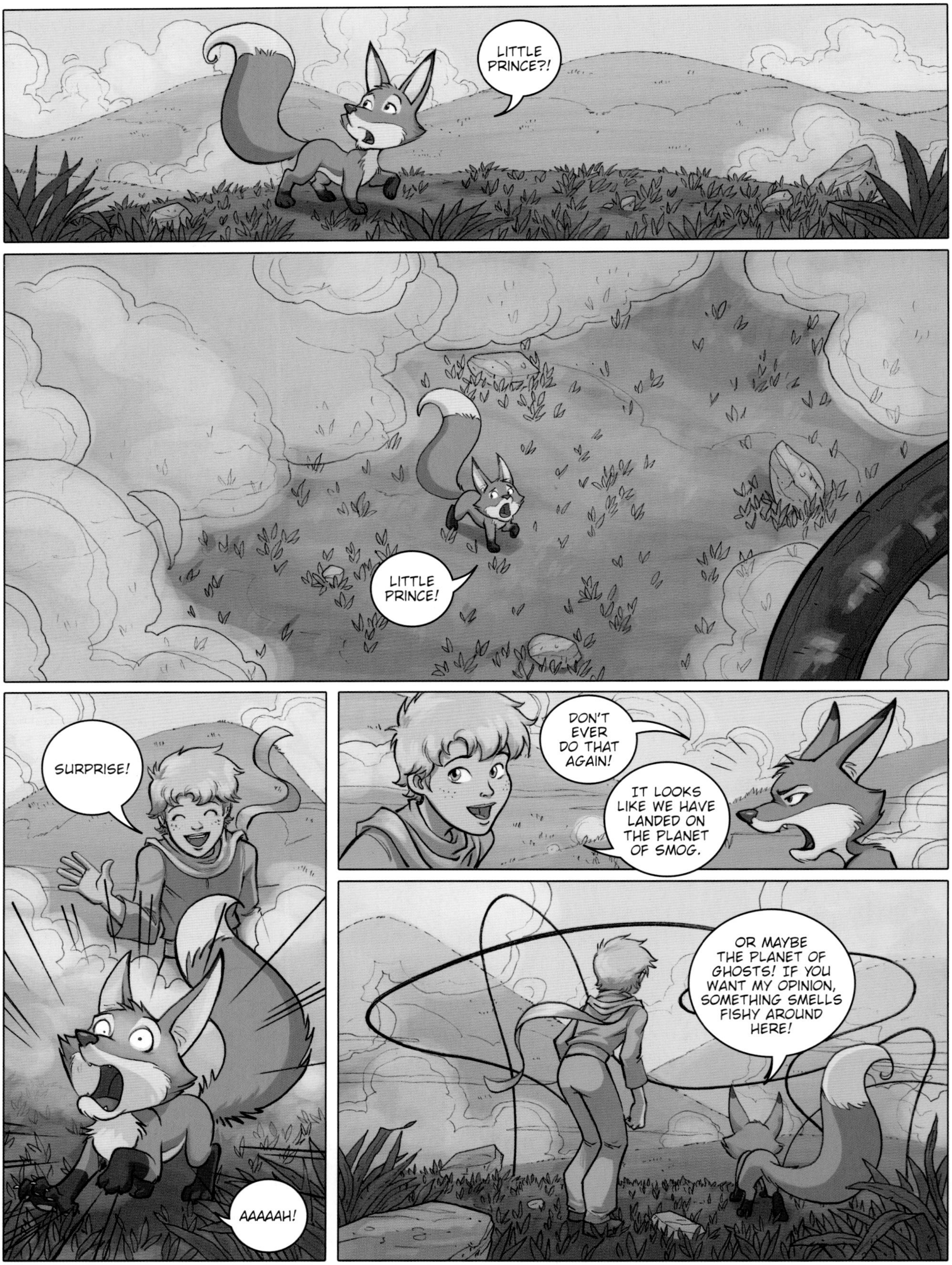
LITTLE PRINCE?!
LITTLE PRINCE!
SURPRISE!
AAAAAH!
DON'T EVER DO THAT AGAIN!
IT LOOKS LIKE WE HAVE LANDED ON THE PLANET OF SMOG.
OR MAYBE THE PLANET OF GHOSTS! IF YOU WANT MY OPINION, SOMETHING SMELLS FISHY AROUND HERE!

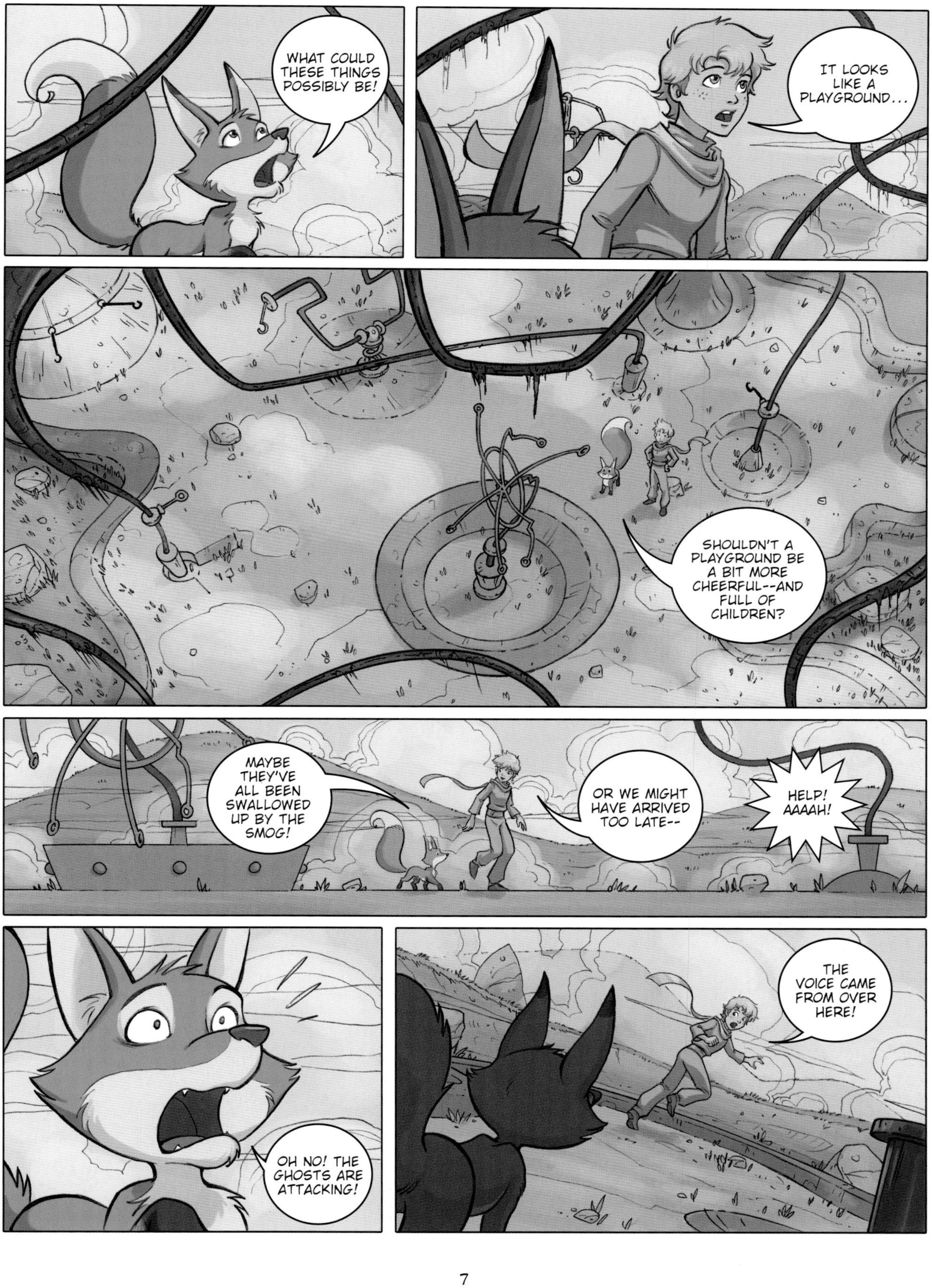
WHAT COULD THESE THINGS POSSIBLY BE!
IT LOOKS LIKE A PLAYGROUND...
SHOULDN'T A PLAYGROUND BE A BIT MORE CHEERFUL--AND FULL OF CHILDREN?
MAYBE THEY'VE ALL BEEN SWALLOWED UP BY THE SMOG!
OR WE MIGHT HAVE ARRIVED TOO LATE--
HELP! AAAAH!
OH NO! THE GHOSTS ARE ATTACKING!
THE VOICE CAME FROM OVER HERE!

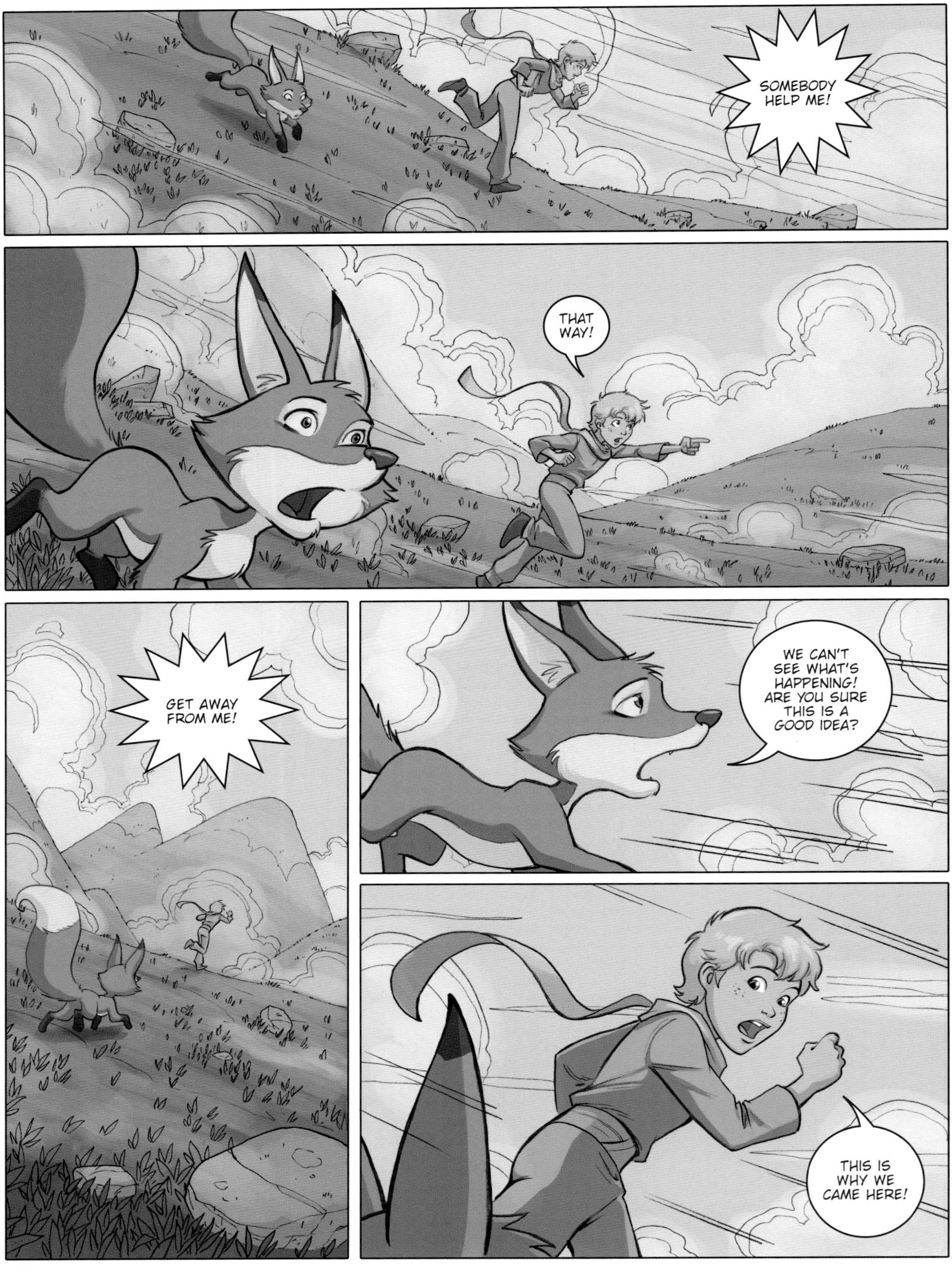
SOMEBODY HELP ME!
THAT WAY!
GET AWAY FROM ME!
WE CAN'T SEE WHAT'S HAPPENING! ARE YOU SURE THIS IS A GOOD IDEA?
THIS IS WHY WE CAME HERE!

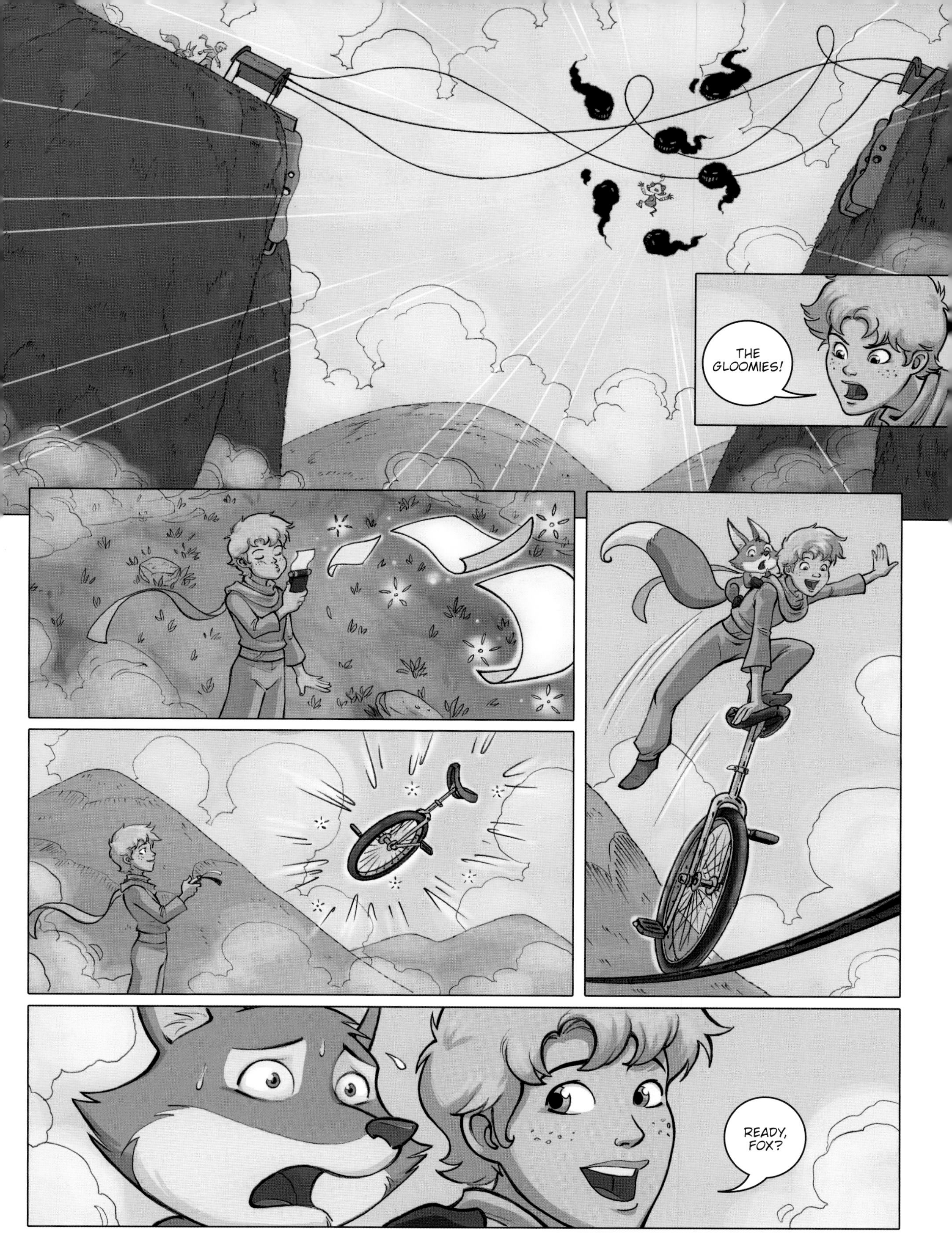
THE GLOOMIES!
READY, FOX?

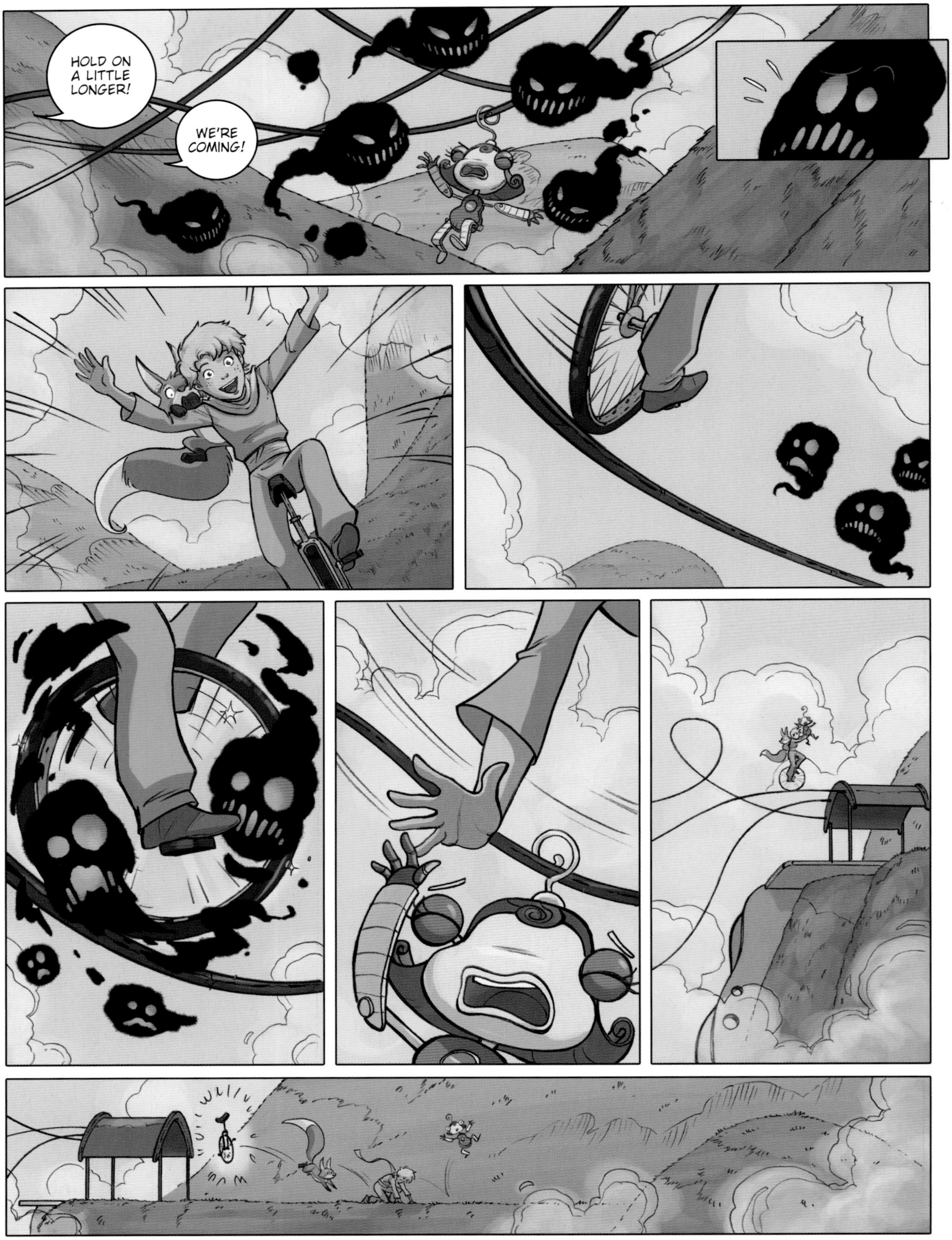
HOLD ON A LITTLE LONGER!
WE'RE COMING!

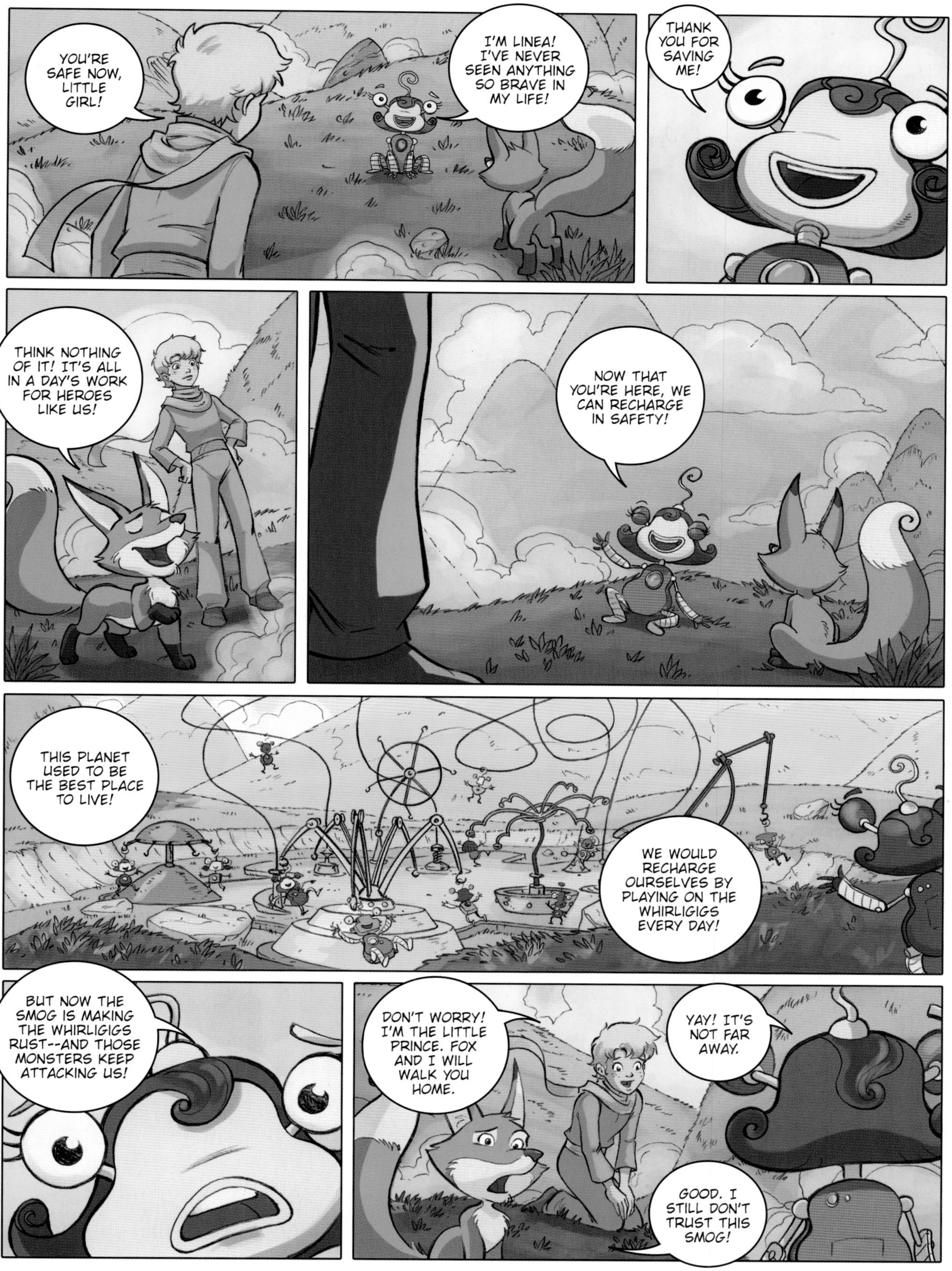
YOU'RE SAFE NOW, LITTLE GIRL!
I'M LINEA! I'VE NEVER SEEN ANYTHING SO BRAVE IN MY LIFE!
THANK YOU FOR SAVING ME!
THINK NOTHING OF IT! IT'S ALL IN A DAY'S WORK FOR HEROES LIKE US!
NOW THAT YOU'RE HERE, WE CAN RECHARGE IN SAFETY!
THIS PLANET USED TO BE THE BEST PLACE TO LIVE!
WE WOULD RECHARGE OURSELVES BY PLAYING ON THE WHIRLIGIGS EVERY DAY!
BUT NOW THE SMOG IS MAKING THE WHIRLIGIGS RUST--AND THOSE MONSTERS KEEP ATTACKING US!
DON'T WORRY! I'M THE LITTLE PRINCE. FOX AND I WILL WALK YOU HOME.
YAY! IT'S NOT FAR AWAY.
GOOD. I STILL DON'T TRUST THIS SMOG!

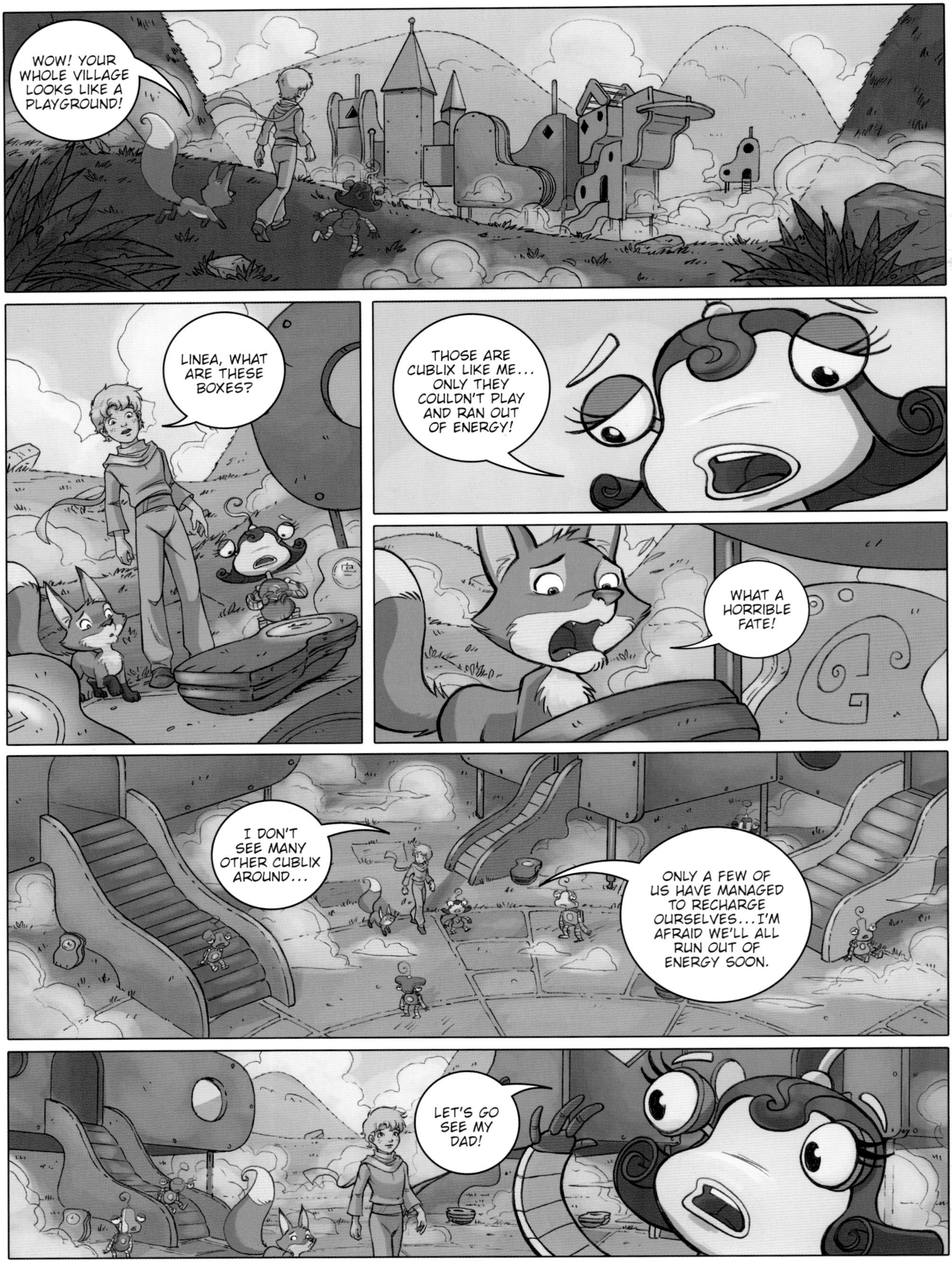
WOW! YOUR WHOLE VILLAGE LOOKS LIKE A PLAYGROUND!
LINEA, WHAT ARE THESE BOXES?
THOSE ARE CUBLIX LIKE ME... ONLY THEY COULDN'T PLAY AND RAN OUT OF ENERGY!
WHAT A HORRIBLE FATE!
I DON'T SEE MANY OTHER CUBLIX AROUND...
ONLY A FEW OF US HAVE MANAGED TO RECHARGE OURSELVES...I'M AFRAID WE'LL ALL RUN OUT OF ENERGY SOON.
LET'S GO SEE MY DAD!

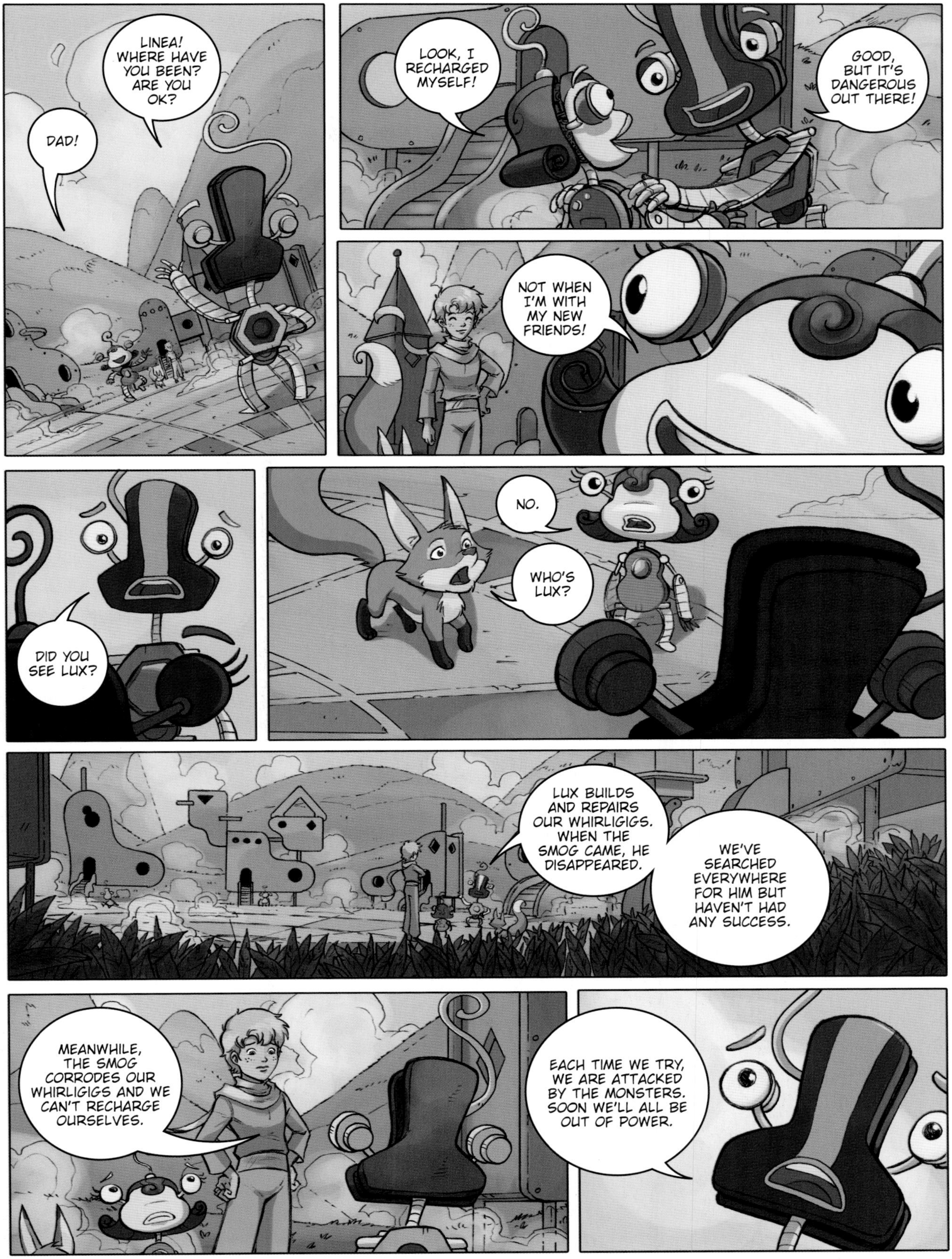
DAD!
LINEA! WHERE HAVE YOU BEEN? ARE YOU OK?
LOOK, I RECHARGED MYSELF!
GOOD, BUT IT'S DANGEROUS OUT THERE!
NOT WHEN I'M WITH MY NEW FRIENDS!
DID YOU SEE LUX?
NO.
WHO'S LUX?
LUX BUILDS AND REPAIRS OUR WHIRLIGIGS. WHEN THE SMOG CAME, HE DISAPPEARED.
WE'VE SEARCHED EVERYWHERE FOR HIM BUT HAVEN'T HAD ANY SUCCESS.
MEANWHILE, THE SMOG CORRODES OUR WHIRLIGIGS AND WE CAN'T RECHARGE OURSELVES.
EACH TIME WE TRY, WE ARE ATTACKED BY THE MONSTERS. SOON WE'LL ALL BE OUT OF POWER.

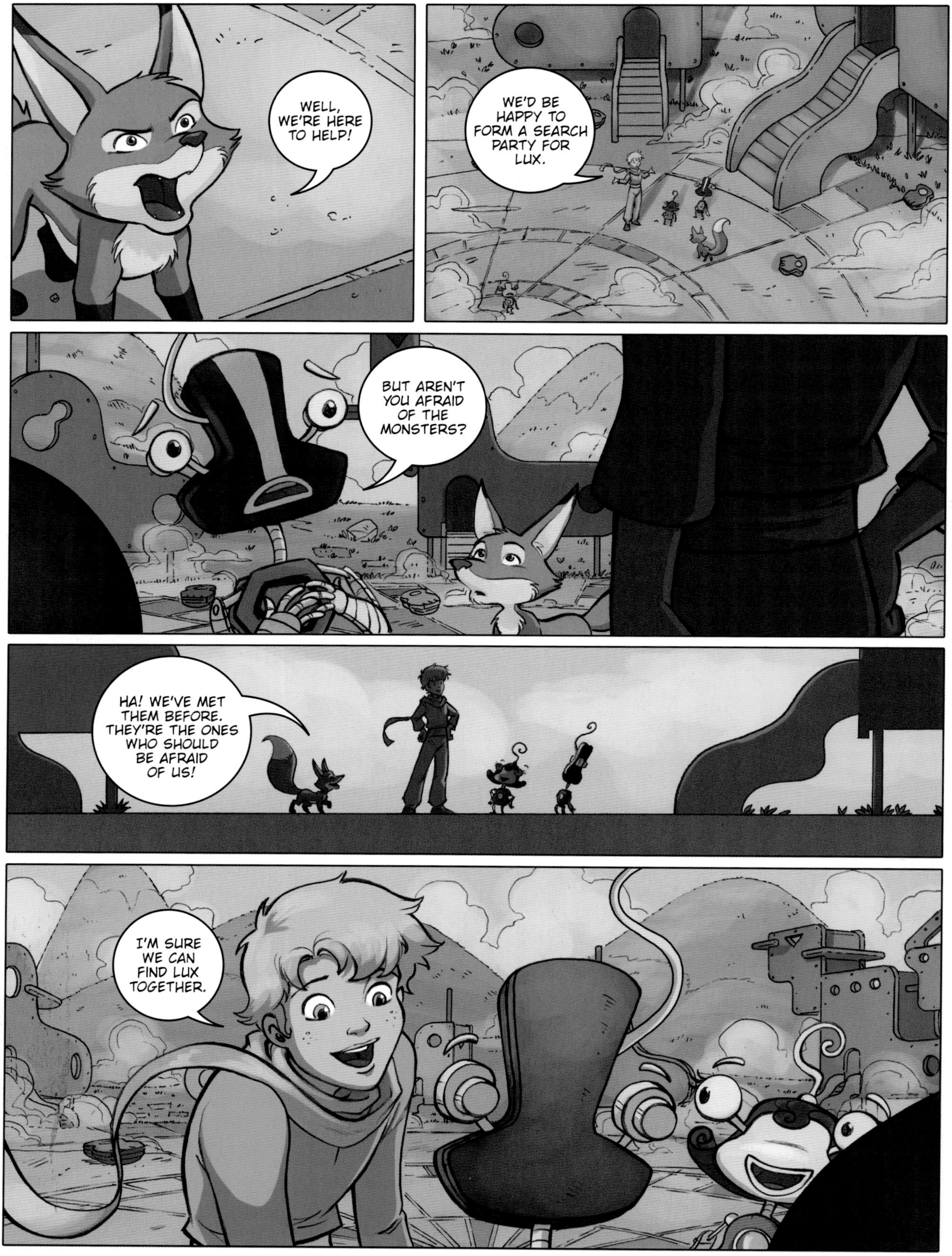
WELL, WE'RE HERE TO HELP!
WE'D BE HAPPY TO FORM A SEARCH PARTY FOR LUX.
BUT AREN'T YOU AFRAID OF THE MONSTERS?
HA! WE'VE MET THEM BEFORE. THEY'RE THE ONES WHO SHOULD BE AFRAID OF US!
I'M SURE WE CAN FIND LUX TOGETHER.

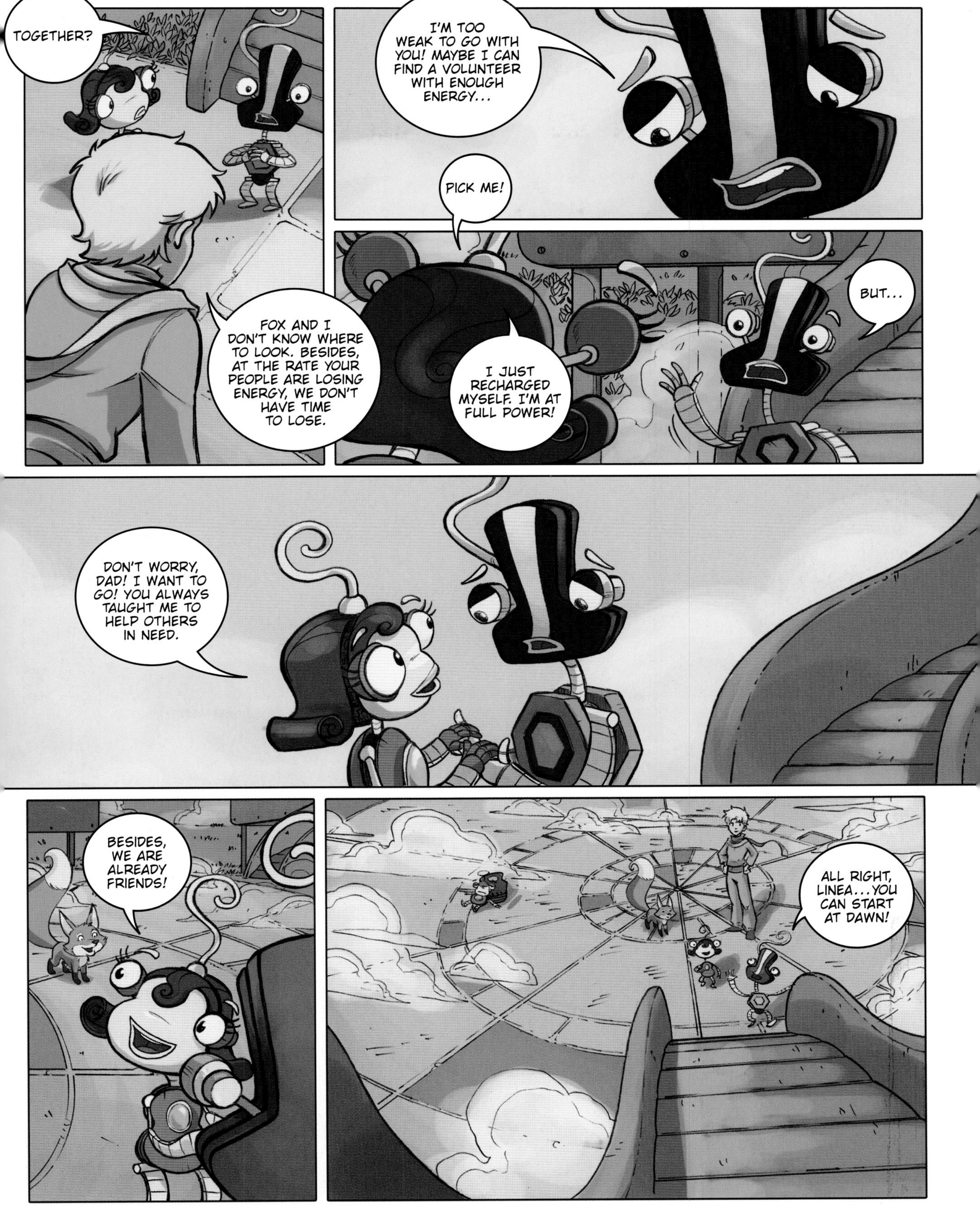
TOGETHER?
FOX AND I DON'T KNOW WHERE TO LOOK. BESIDES, AT THE RATE YOUR PEOPLE ARE LOSING ENERGY, WE DON'T HAVE TIME TO LOSE.
I'M TOO WEAK TO GO WITH YOU! MAYBE I CAN FIND A VOLUNTEER WITH ENOUGH ENERGY...
PICK ME!
I JUST RECHARGED MYSELF. I'M AT FULL POWER!
BUT...
DON'T WORRY, DAD! I WANT TO GO! YOU ALWAYS TAUGHT ME TO HELP OTHERS IN NEED.
BESIDES, WE ARE ALREADY FRIENDS!
ALL RIGHT, LINEA...YOU CAN START AT DAWN!

THERE!
I'M DONE!

ARE YOU
SURE ABOUT
THAT?

I'M NOT
SURE YOU'VE
MADE ENOUGH
PADLOCKS...
HSSS...

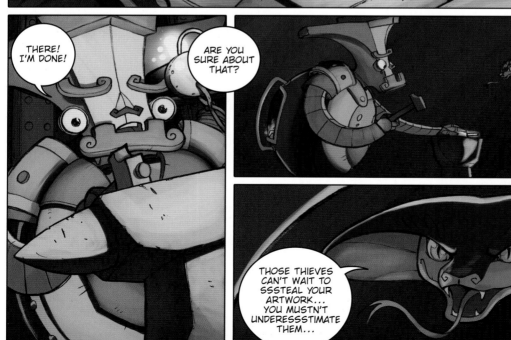

THOSE THIEVES
CAN'T WAIT TO
SSSTEAL YOUR
ARTWORK...
YOU MUSTN'T
UNDERESSSTIMATE
THEM...

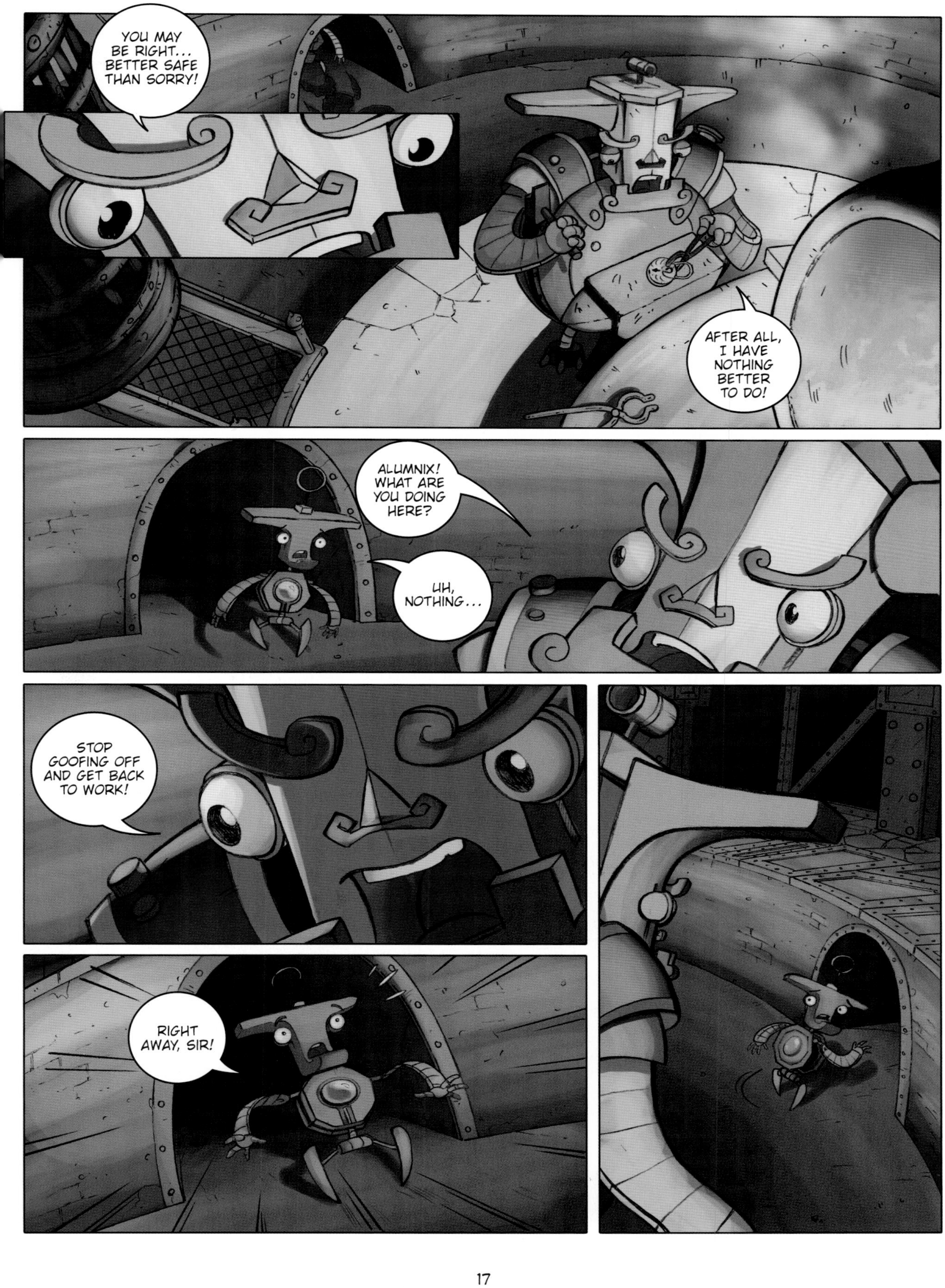
YOU MAY BE RIGHT... BETTER SAFE THAN SORRY!
AFTER ALL, I HAVE NOTHING BETTER TO DO!
ALUMNIX! WHAT ARE YOU DOING HERE?
UH, NOTHING...
STOP GOOFING OFF AND GET BACK TO WORK!
RIGHT AWAY, SIR!

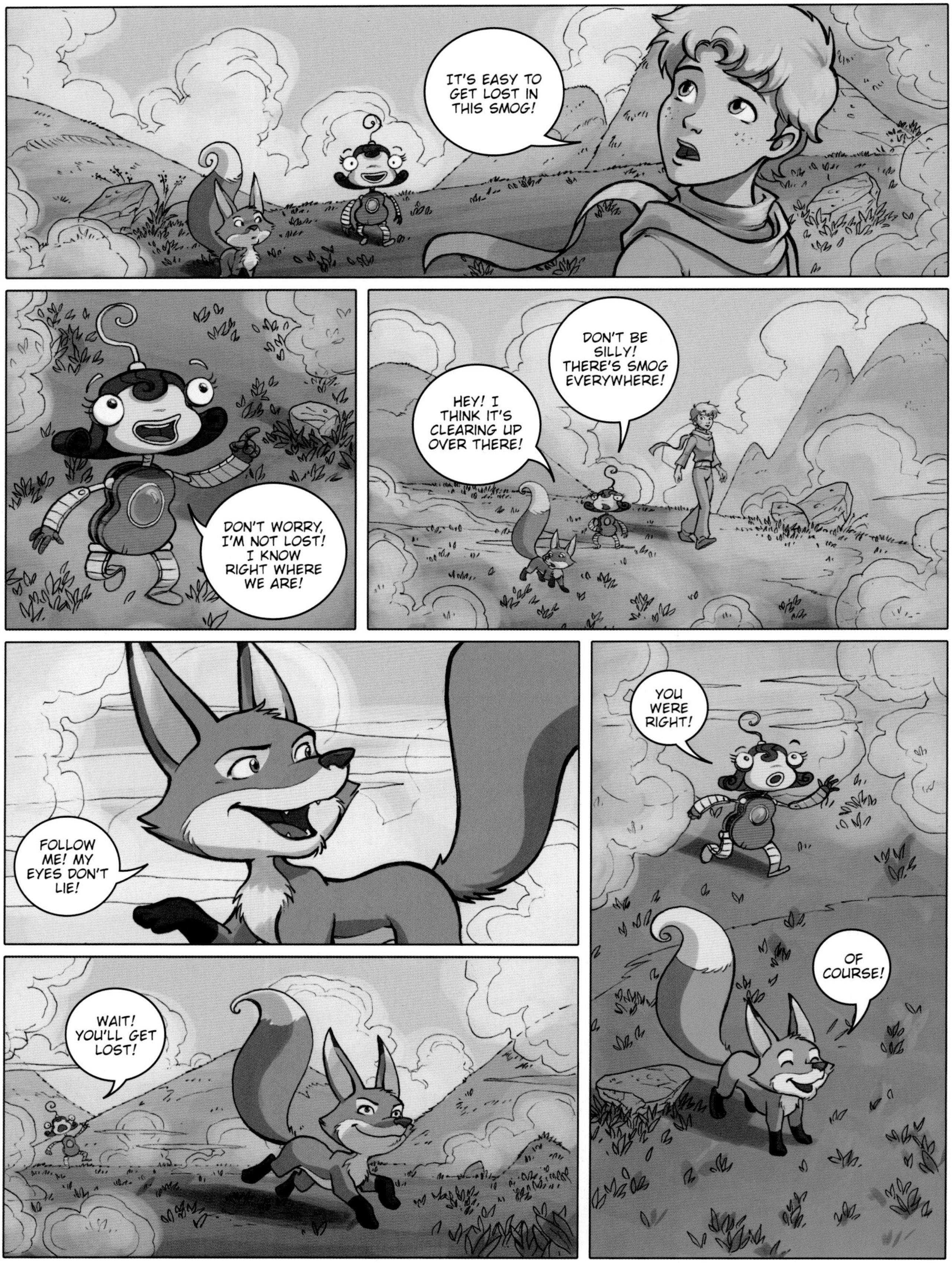
IT'S EASY TO GET LOST IN THIS SMOG!
DON'T WORRY, I'M NOT LOST! I KNOW RIGHT WHERE WE ARE!
HEY! I THINK IT'S CLEARING UP OVER THERE!
DON'T BE SILLY! THERE'S SMOG EVERYWHERE!
FOLLOW ME! MY EYES DON'T LIE!
WAIT! YOU'LL GET LOST!
YOU WERE RIGHT!
OF COURSE!

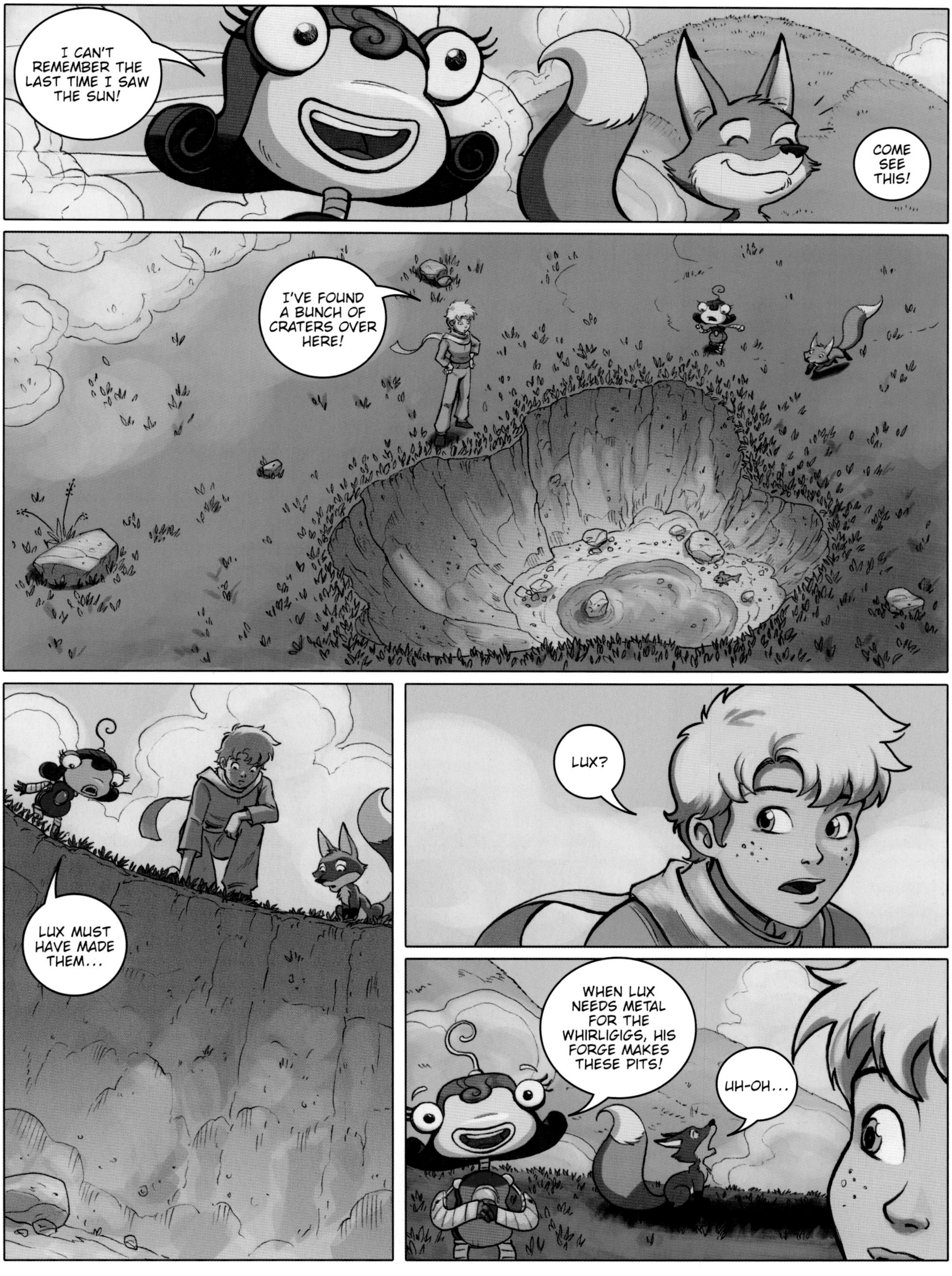
I CAN'T REMEMBER THE LAST TIME I SAW THE SUN!
COME SEE THIS!
I'VE FOUND A BUNCH OF CRATERS OVER HERE!
LUX MUST HAVE MADE THEM...
LUX?
WHEN LUX NEEDS METAL FOR THE WHIRLIGIGS, HIS FORGE MAKES THESE PITS!
UH-OH...

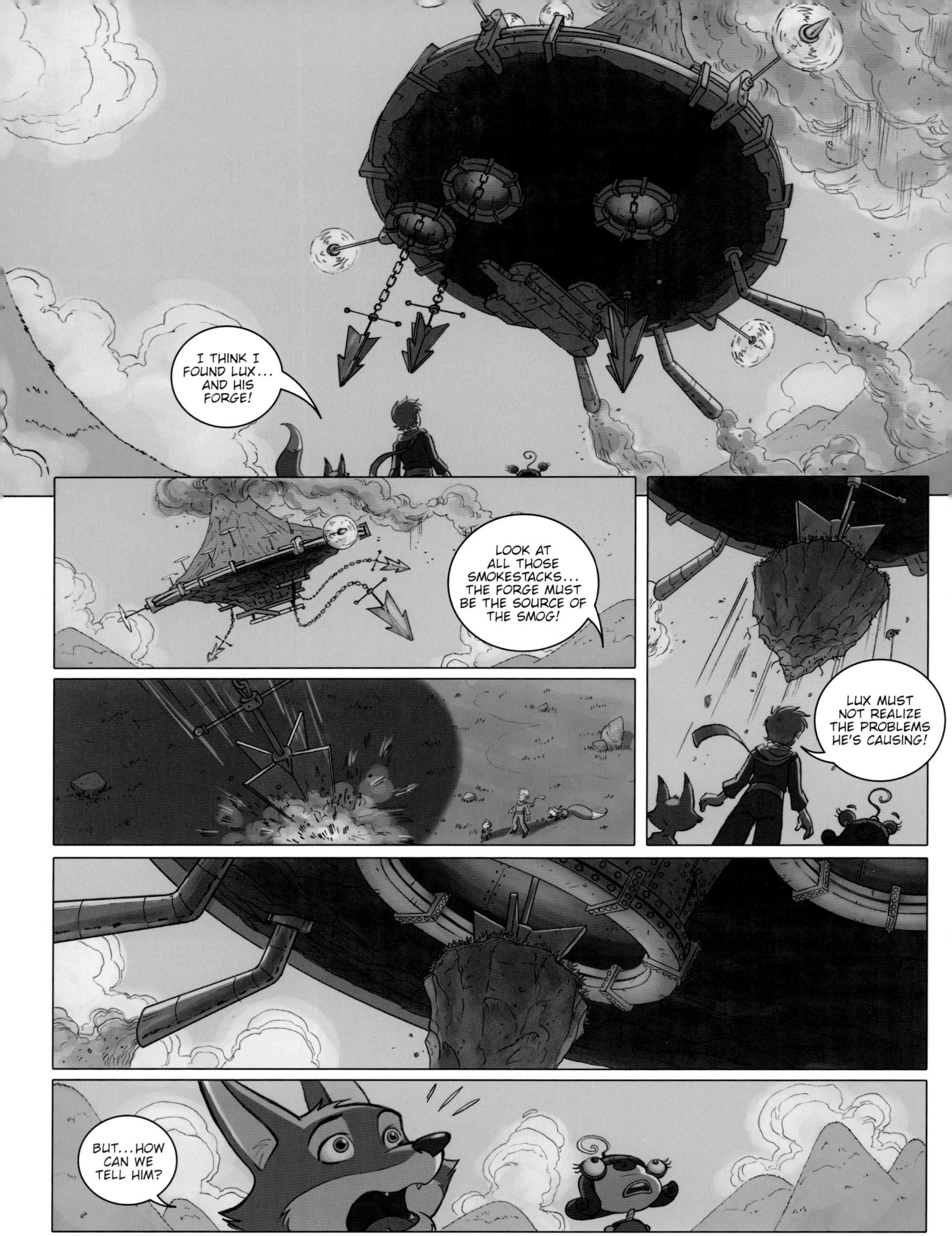
I THINK I FOUND LUX... AND HIS FORGE!
LOOK AT ALL THOSE SMOKESTACKS... THE FORGE MUST BE THE SOURCE OF THE SMOG!
LUX MUST NOT REALIZE THE PROBLEMS HE'S CAUSING!
BUT...HOW CAN WE TELL HIM?

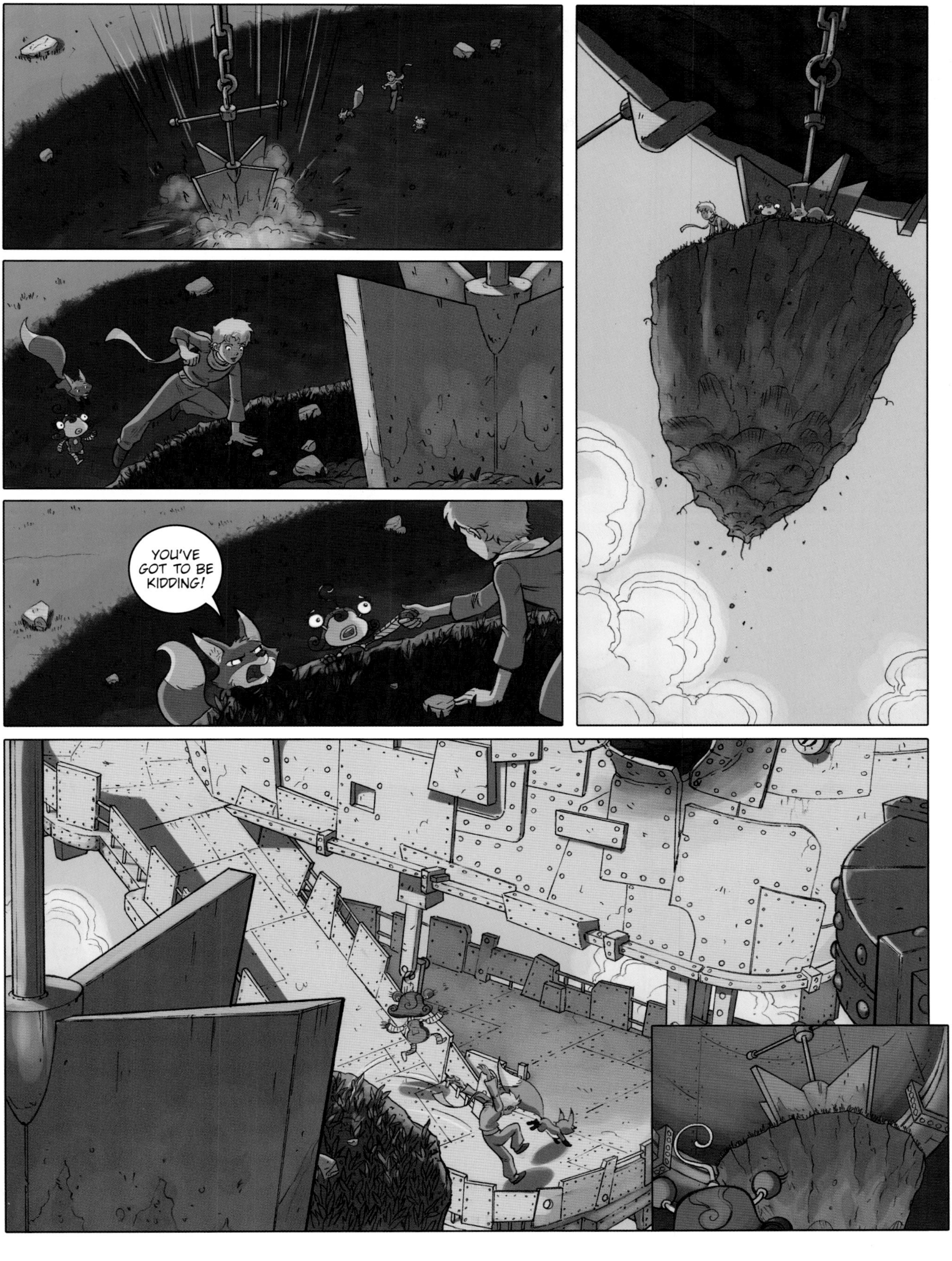
YOU'VE GOT TO BE KIDDING!

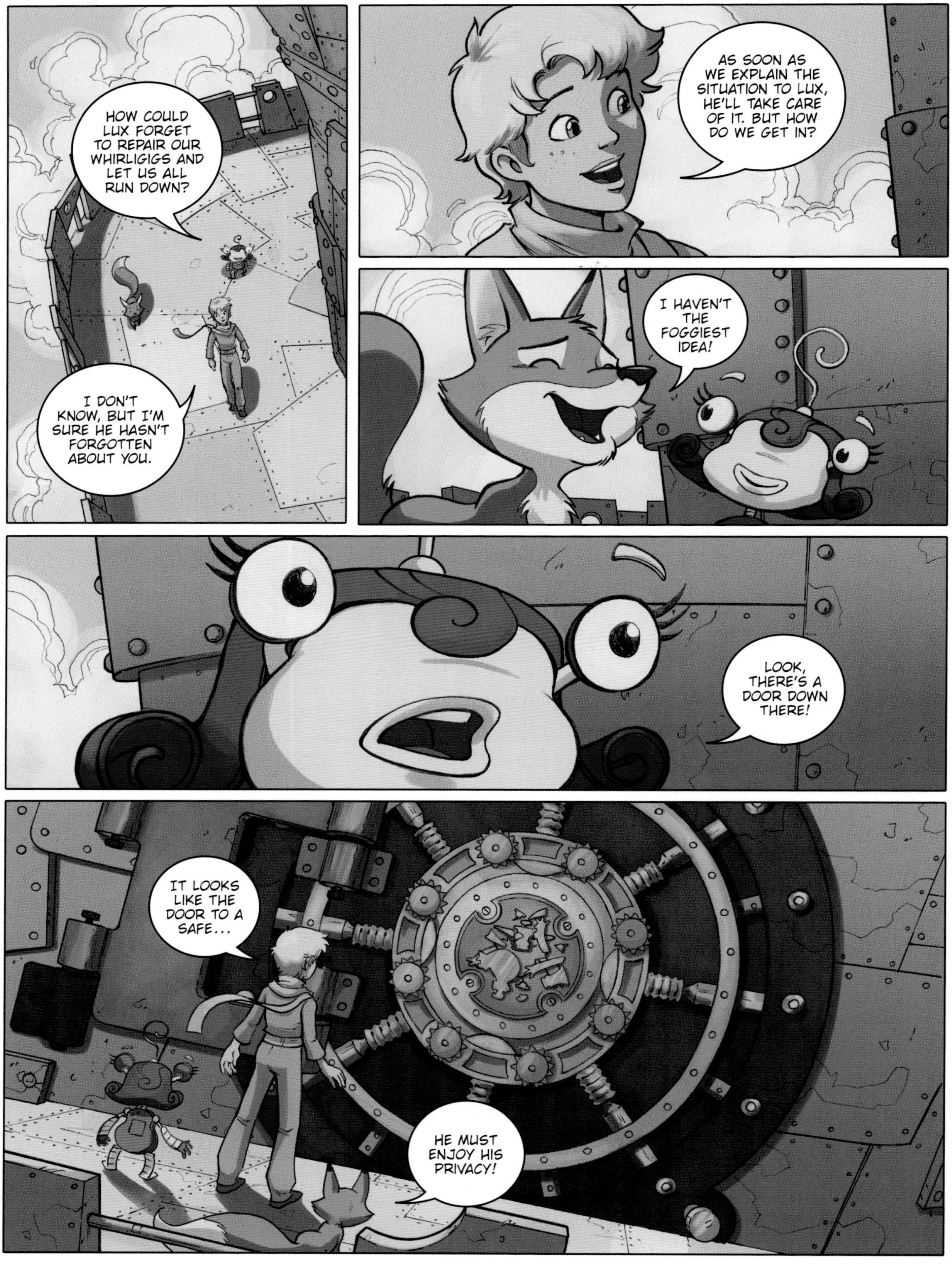
HOW COULD LUX FORGET TO REPAIR OUR WHIRLIGIGS AND LET US ALL RUN DOWN?
I DON'T KNOW, BUT I'M SURE HE HASN'T FORGOTTEN ABOUT YOU.
AS SOON AS WE EXPLAIN THE SITUATION TO LUX, HE'LL TAKE CARE OF IT. BUT HOW DO WE GET IN?
I HAVEN'T THE FOGGIEST IDEA!
LOOK, THERE'S A DOOR DOWN THERE!
IT LOOKS LIKE THE DOOR TO A SAFE...
HE MUST ENJOY HIS PRIVACY!

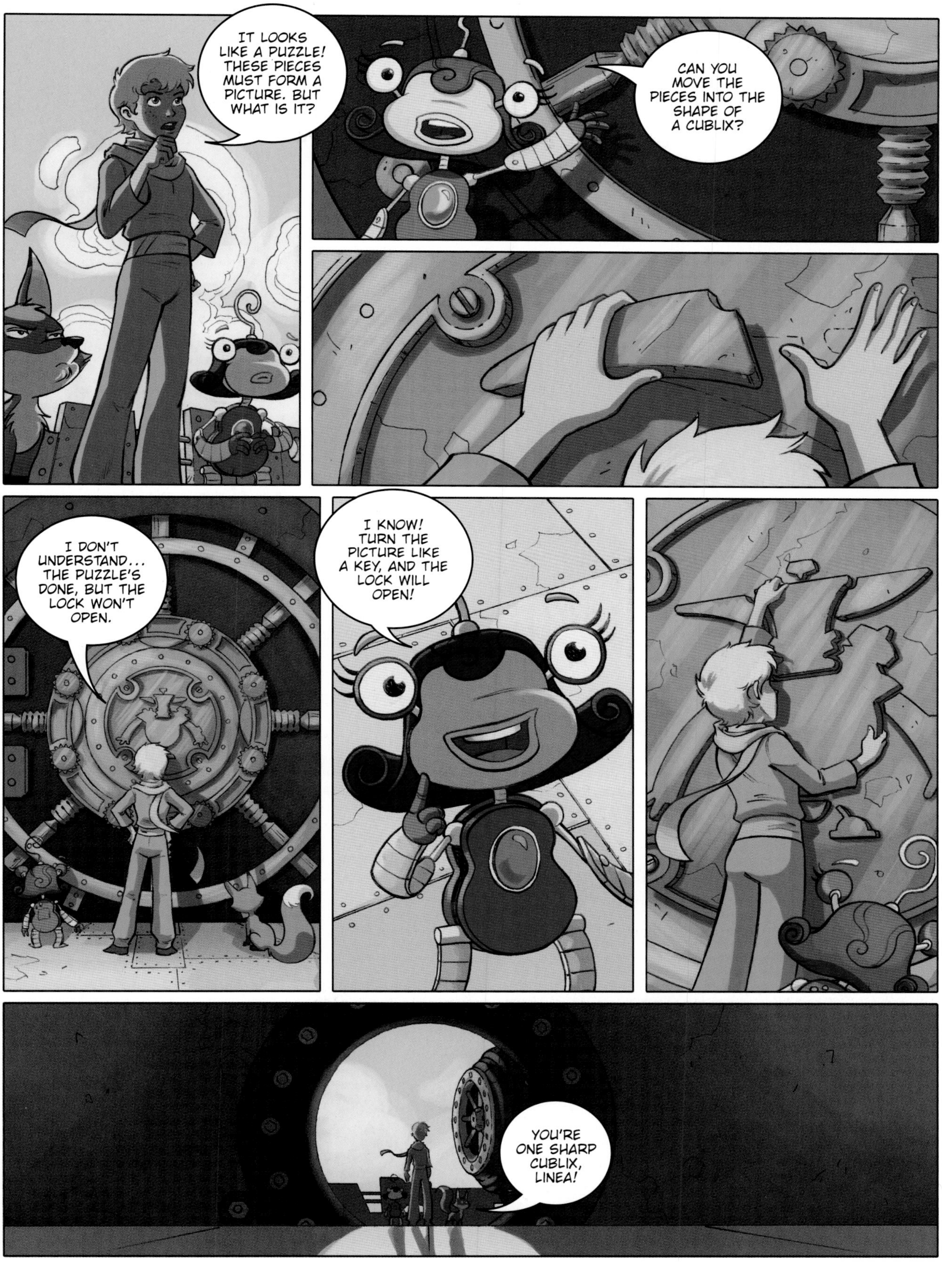
IT LOOKS LIKE A PUZZLE! THESE PIECES MUST FORM A PICTURE. BUT WHAT IS IT?
CAN YOU MOVE THE PIECES INTO THE SHAPE OF A CUBLIX?
I DON'T UNDERSTAND... THE PUZZLE'S DONE, BUT THE LOCK WON'T OPEN.
I KNOW! TURN THE PICTURE LIKE A KEY, AND THE LOCK WILL OPEN!
YOU'RE ONE SHARP CUBLIX, LINEA!

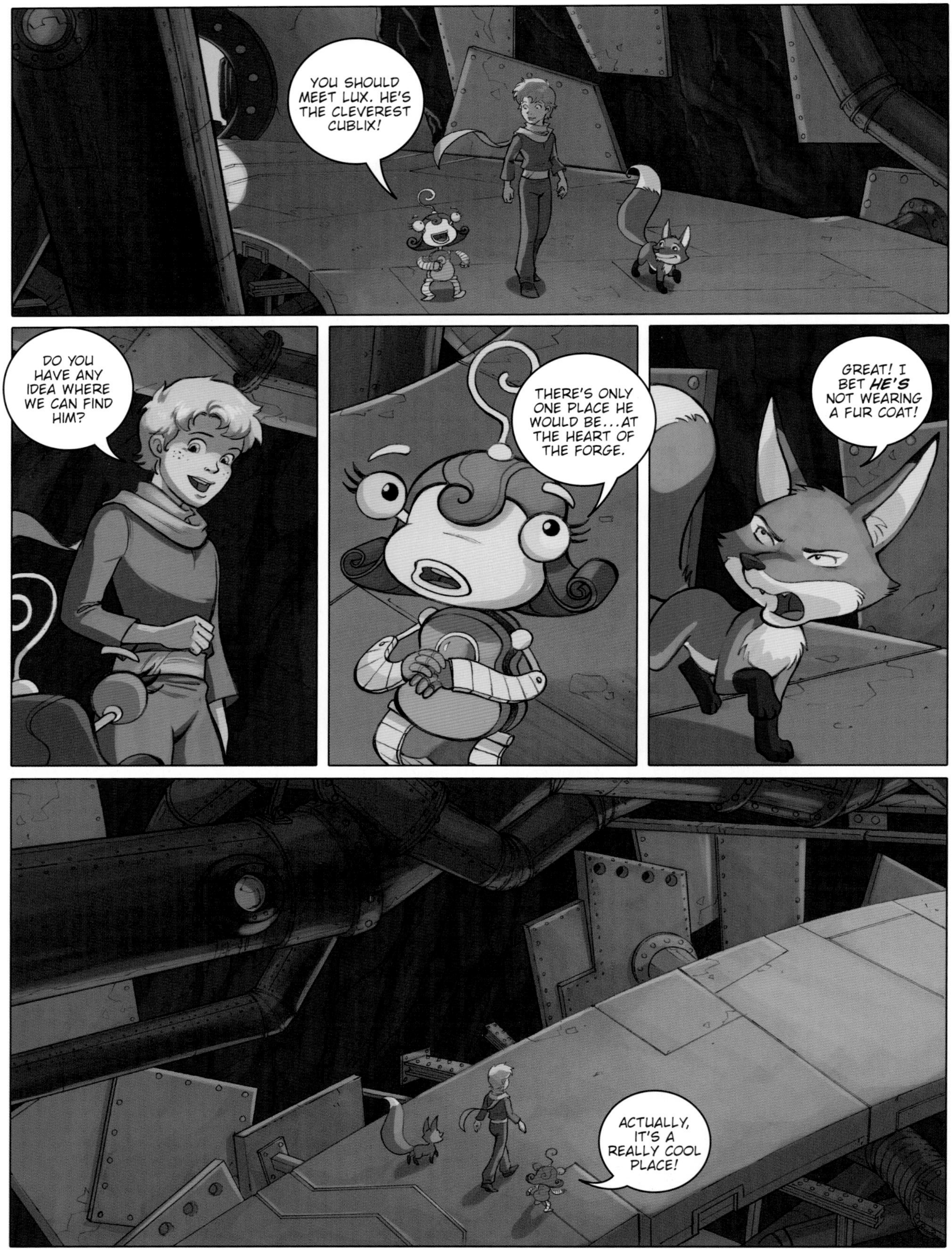
YOU SHOULD MEET LUX. HE'S THE CLEVEREST CUBLIX!
DO YOU HAVE ANY IDEA WHERE WE CAN FIND HIM?
THERE'S ONLY ONE PLACE HE WOULD BE...AT THE HEART OF THE FORGE.
GREAT! I BET HE'S NOT WEARING A FUR COAT!
ACTUALLY, IT'S A REALLY COOL PLACE!

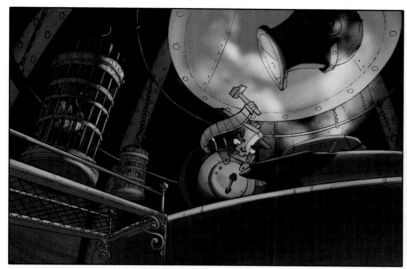

WHAT?!

NICE TO MEET YOU! I'M--

INTRUDERS! I KNOW WHY YOU'RE HERE!

YOU WANT TO STEAL MY TREASURES!

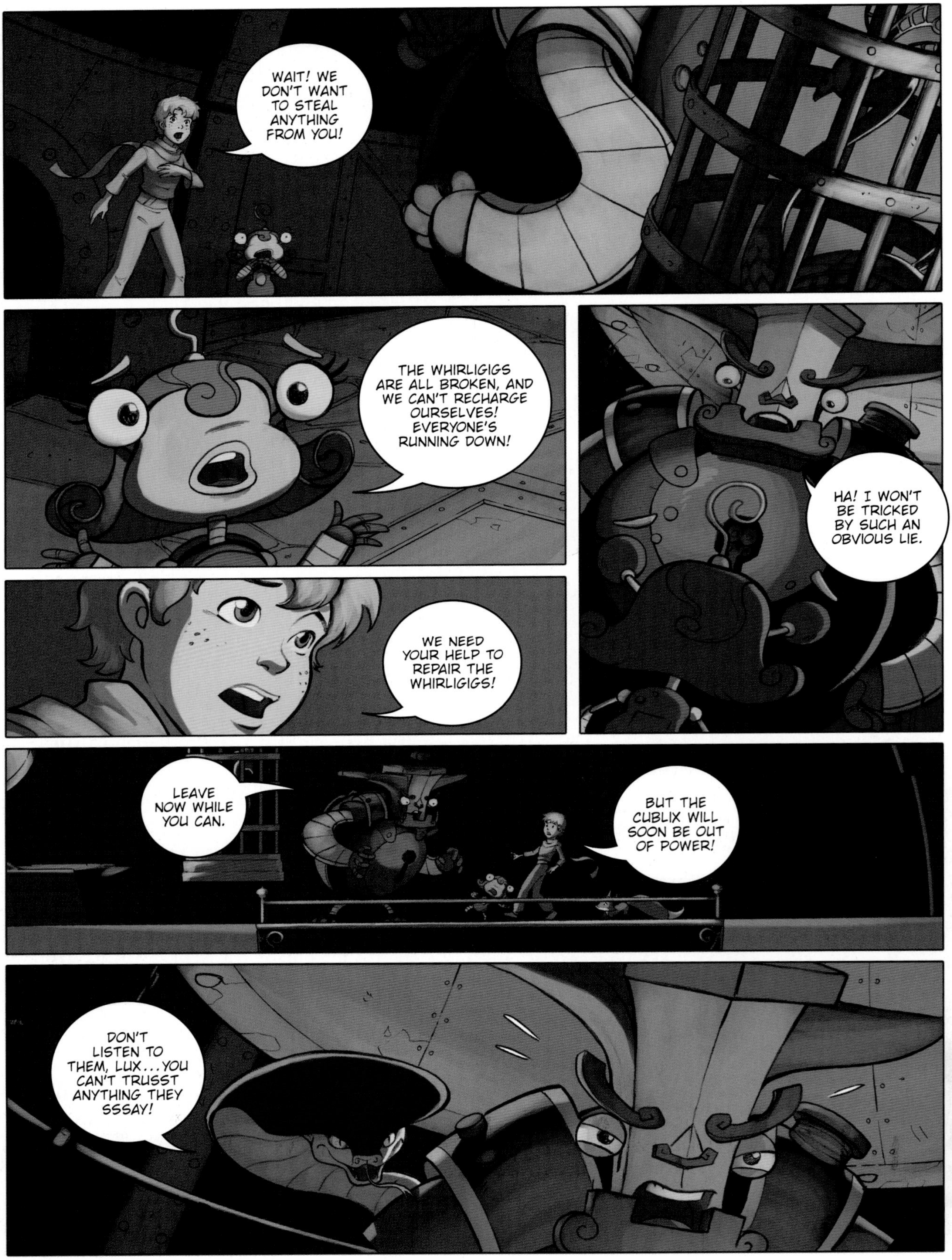

WAIT! WE DON'T WANT TO STEAL ANYTHING FROM YOU!
THE WHIRLIGIGS ARE ALL BROKEN, AND WE CAN'T RECHARGE OURSELVES! EVERYONE'S RUNNING DOWN!
WE NEED YOUR HELP TO REPAIR THE WHIRLIGIGS!
HA! I WON'T BE TRICKED BY SUCH AN OBVIOUS LIE.
LEAVE NOW WHILE YOU CAN.
BUT THE CUBLIX WILL SOON BE OUT OF POWER!
DON'T LISTEN TO THEM, LUX...YOU CAN'T TRUSST ANYTHING THEY SSSAY!

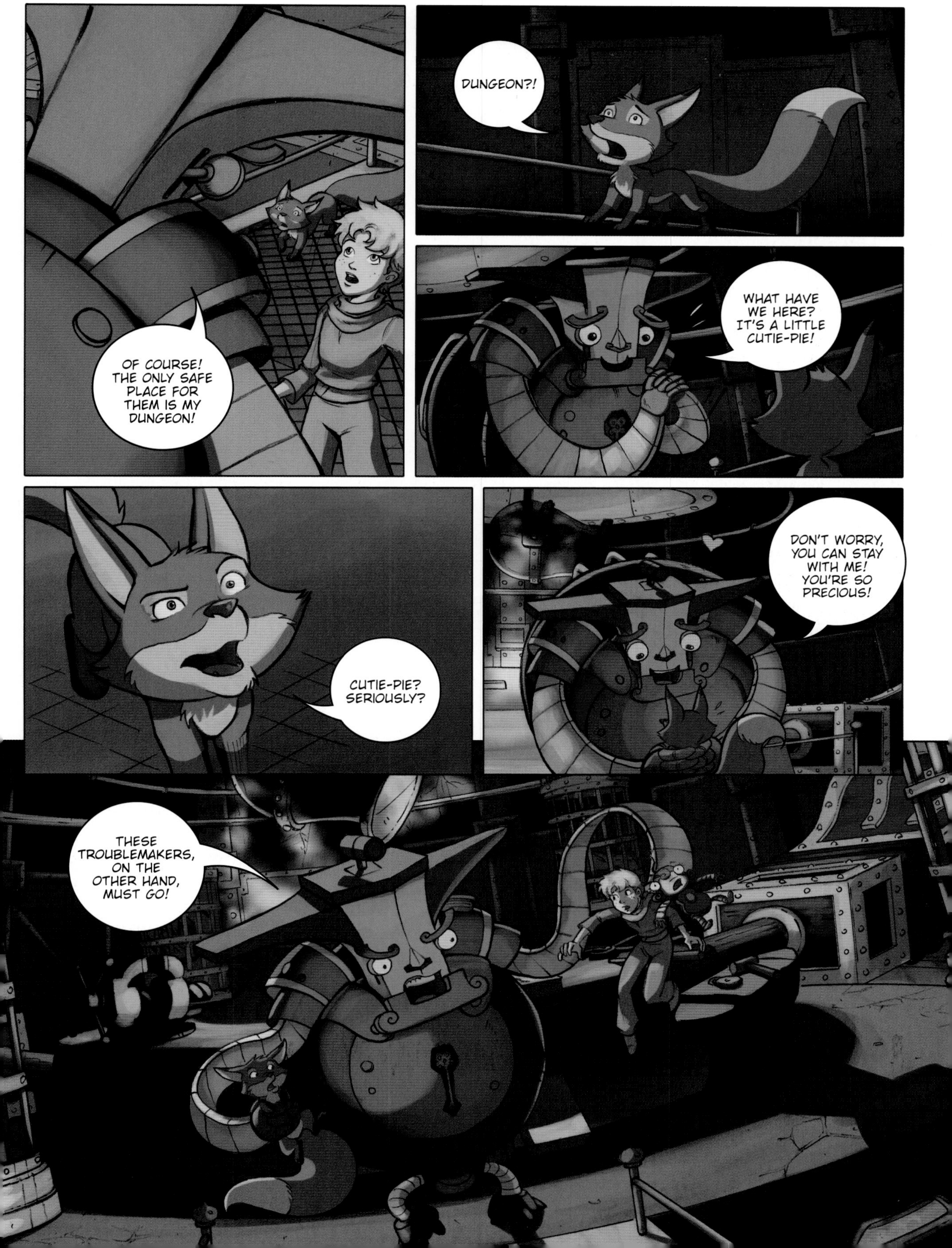
OF COURSE! THE ONLY SAFE PLACE FOR THEM IS MY DUNGEON!
DUNGEON?!
WHAT HAVE WE HERE? IT'S A LITTLE CUTIE-PIE!
CUTIE-PIE? SERIOUSLY?
DON'T WORRY, YOU CAN STAY WITH ME! YOU'RE SO PRECIOUS!
THESE TROUBLEMAKERS, ON THE OTHER HAND, MUST GO!

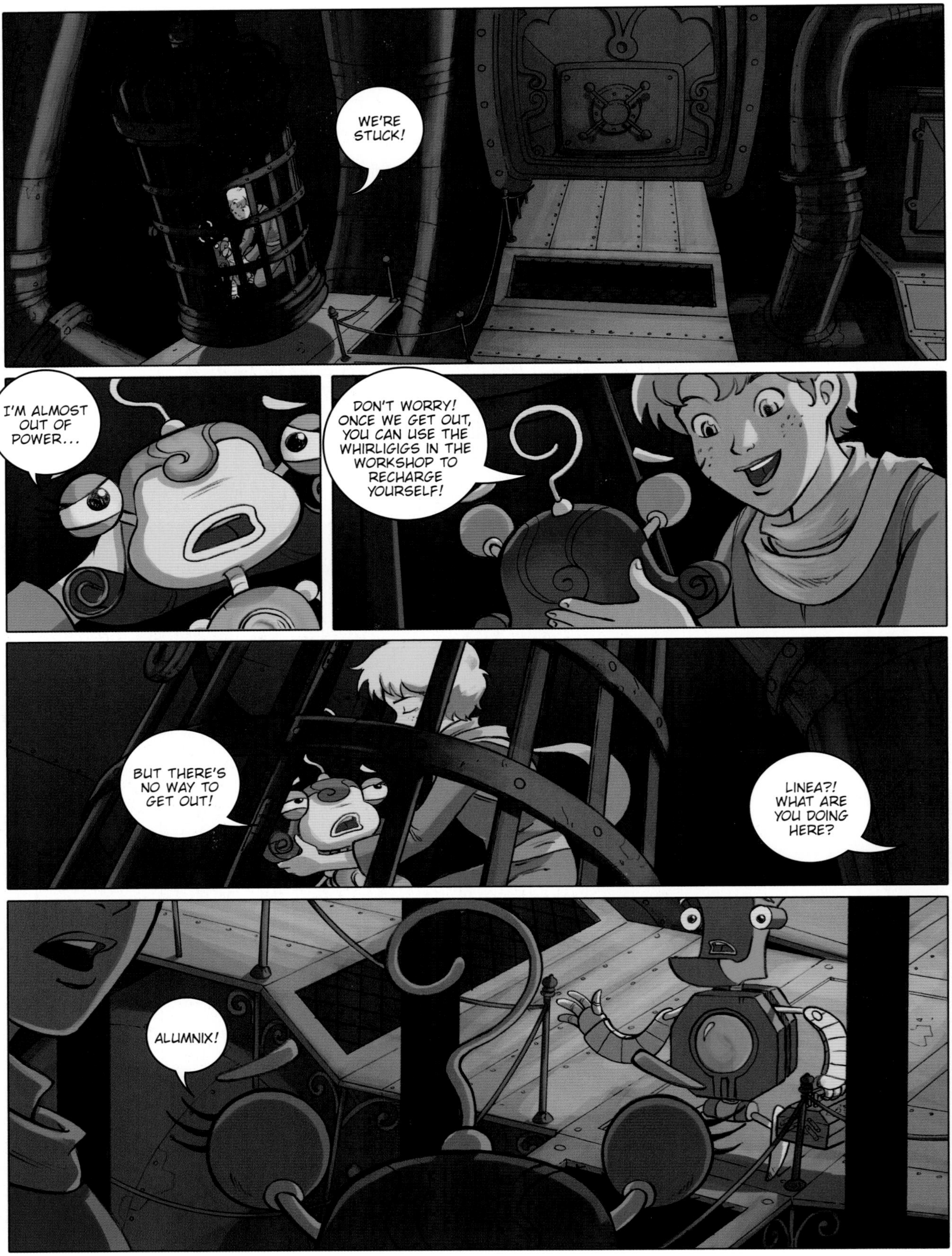
WE'RE STUCK!
I'M ALMOST OUT OF POWER...
DON'T WORRY! ONCE WE GET OUT, YOU CAN USE THE WHIRLIGIGS IN THE WORKSHOP TO RECHARGE YOURSELF!
BUT THERE'S NO WAY TO GET OUT!
LINEA?! WHAT ARE YOU DOING HERE?
ALUMNIX!

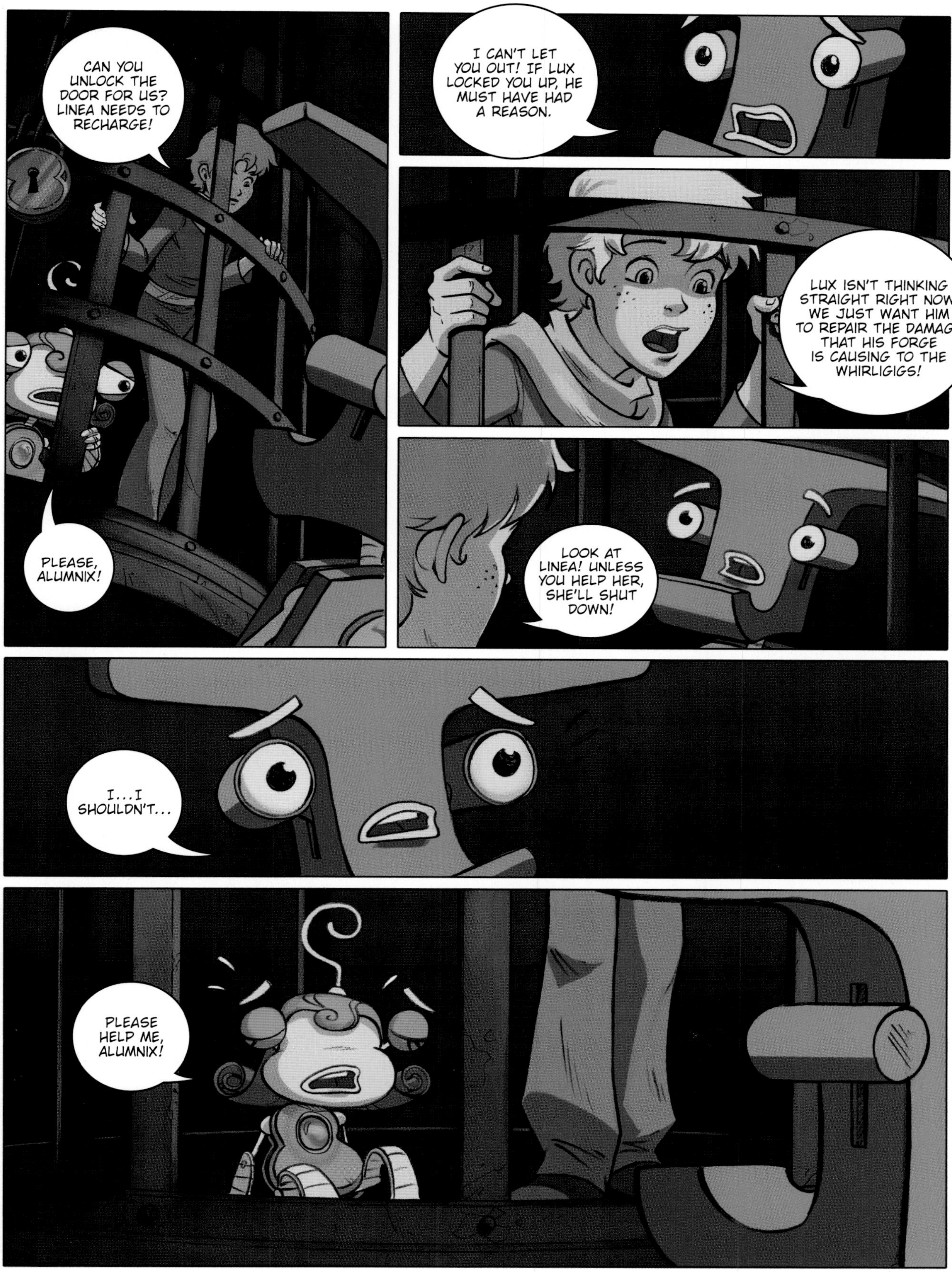
CAN YOU UNLOCK THE DOOR FOR US? LINEA NEEDS TO RECHARGE!
PLEASE, ALUMNIX!
I CAN'T LET YOU OUT! IF LUX LOCKED YOU UP, HE MUST HAVE HAD A REASON.
LUX ISN'T THINKING STRAIGHT RIGHT NOW. WE JUST WANT HIM TO REPAIR THE DAMAGE THAT HIS FORGE IS CAUSING TO THE WHIRLIGIGS!
LOOK AT LINEA! UNLESS YOU HELP HER, SHE'LL SHUT DOWN!
I...I SHOULDN'T...
PLEASE HELP ME, ALUMNIX!

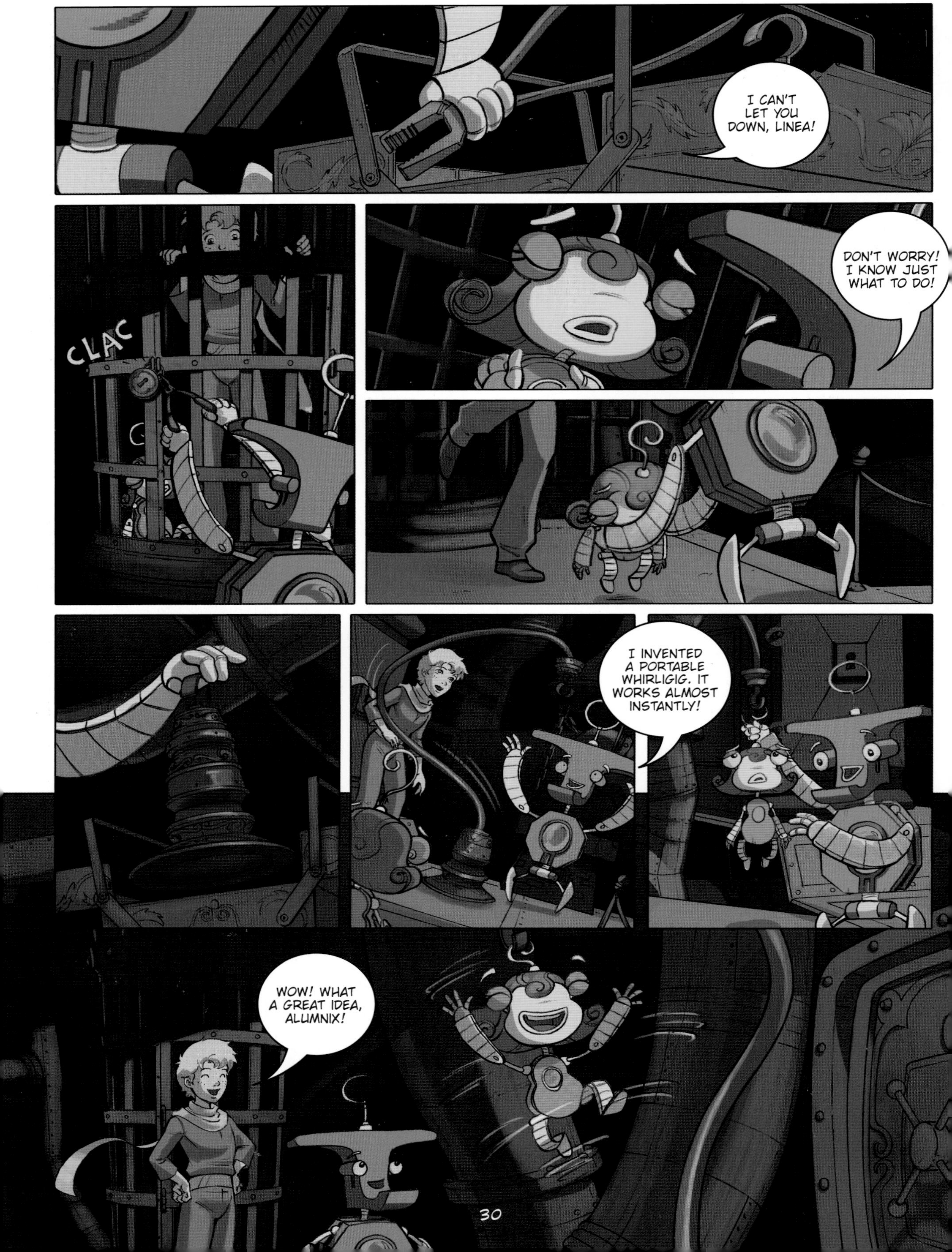
I CAN'T LET YOU DOWN, LINEA!
CLAC
DON'T WORRY! I KNOW JUST WHAT TO DO!
I INVENTED A PORTABLE WHIRLIGIG. IT WORKS ALMOST INSTANTLY!
WOW! WHAT A GREAT IDEA, ALUMNIX!

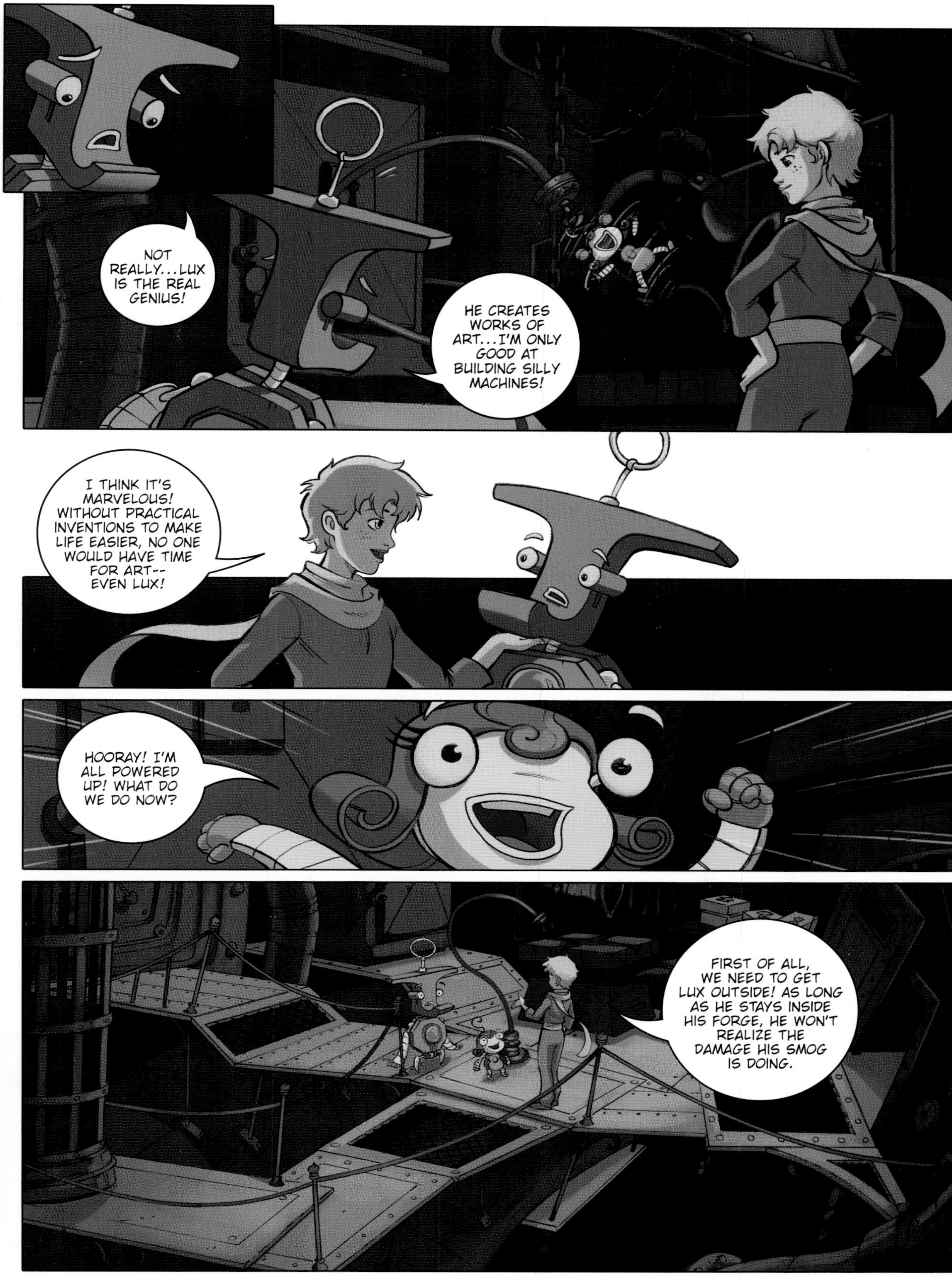
NOT REALLY...LUX IS THE REAL GENIUS!
HE CREATES WORKS OF ART...I'M ONLY GOOD AT BUILDING SILLY MACHINES!
I THINK IT'S MARVELOUS! WITHOUT PRACTICAL INVENTIONS TO MAKE LIFE EASIER, NO ONE WOULD HAVE TIME FOR ART-- EVEN LUX!
HOORAY! I'M ALL POWERED UP! WHAT DO WE DO NOW?
FIRST OF ALL, WE NEED TO GET LUX OUTSIDE! AS LONG AS HE STAYS INSIDE HIS FORGE, HE WON'T REALIZE THE DAMAGE HIS SMOG IS DOING.

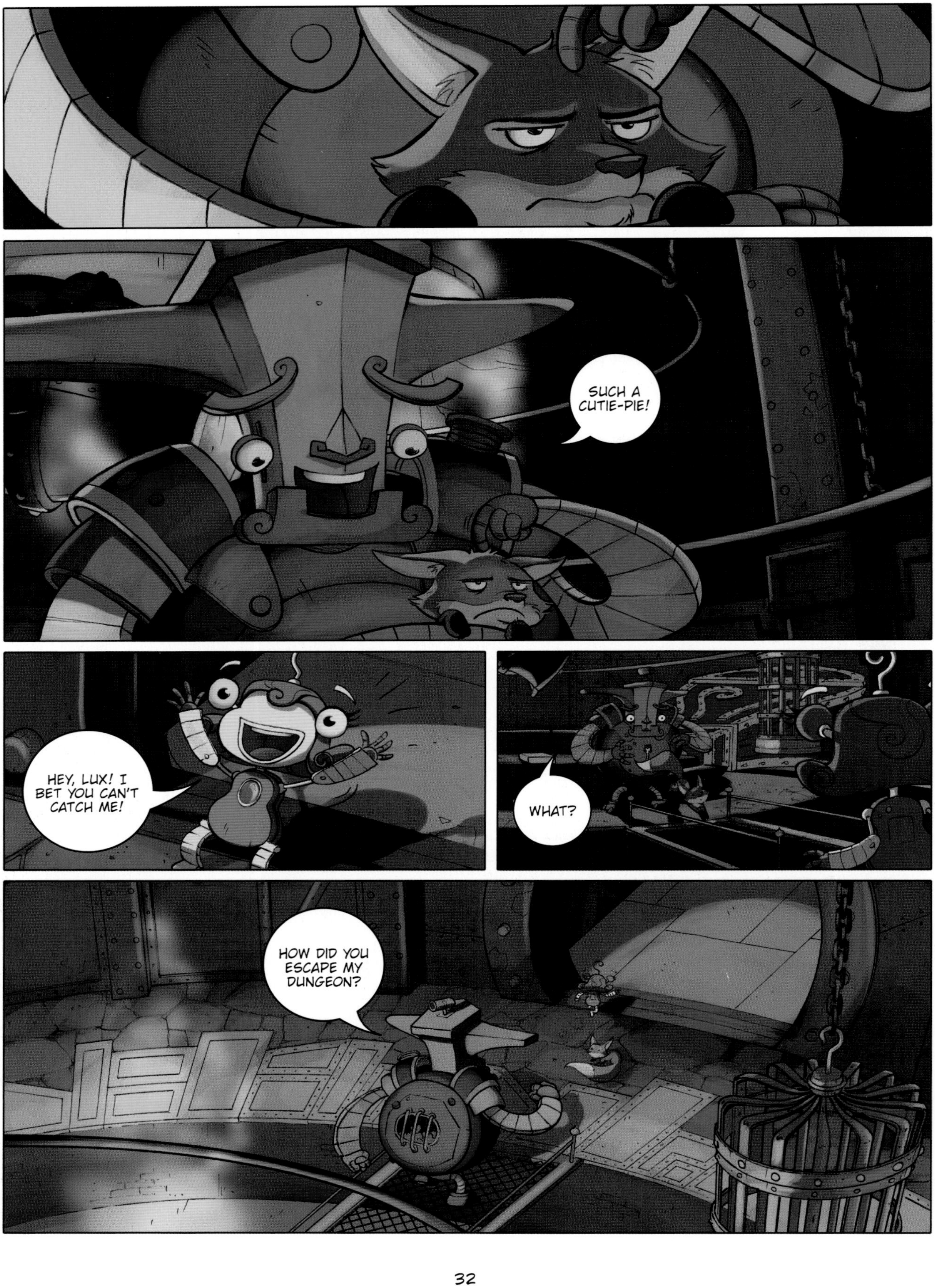
SUCH A CUTIE-PIE!
HEY, LUX! I BET YOU CAN'T CATCH ME!
WHAT?
HOW DID YOU ESCAPE MY DUNGEON?

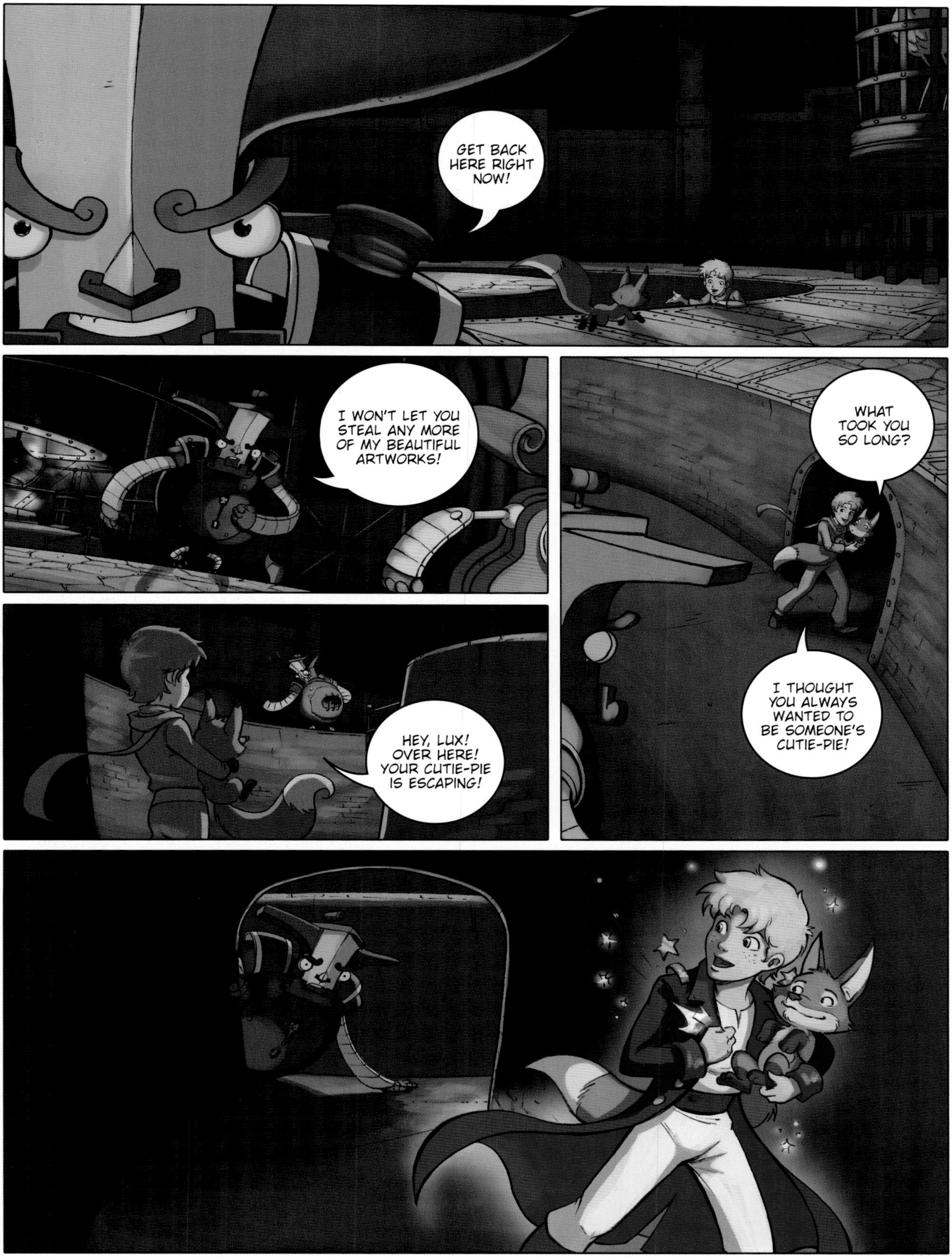
GET BACK HERE RIGHT NOW!
I WON'T LET YOU STEAL ANY MORE OF MY BEAUTIFUL ARTWORKS!
WHAT TOOK YOU SO LONG?
I THOUGHT YOU ALWAYS WANTED TO BE SOMEONE'S CUTIE-PIE!
HEY, LUX! OVER HERE! YOUR CUTIE-PIE IS ESCAPING!

SSSTOP! CAN'T YOU SSSEE IT'S JUST A TRICK! IF YOU LEAVE NOW...
...THEY'LL COME BACK AND STEAL YOUR PRECIOUSSS WORKS OF ART!
BUT I CAN'T LET THEM ESCAPE...
DON'T BE SURPRISED IF ALL YOUR ARTWORK IS GONE WHEN YOU RETURN!
DON'T LISTEN TO HIM!
WE DON'T CARE ABOUT YOUR ARTWORK--THERE ARE MORE IMPORTANT THINGS AT STAKE HERE!
LITTLE PRINCE! DON'T GET THE GIANT CUBLIX MAD!
WHAT?! NOTHING'S MORE IMPORTANT THAN MY ART!

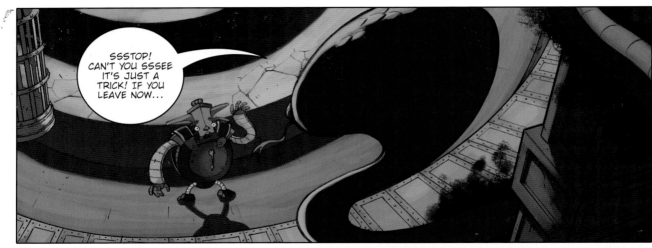

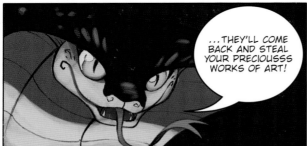

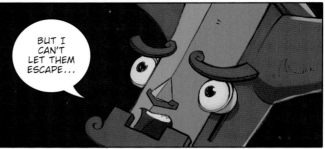

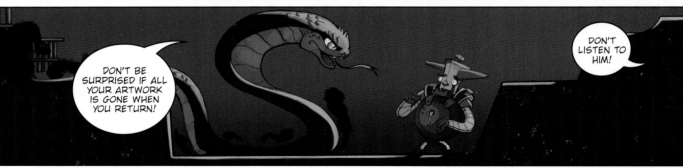

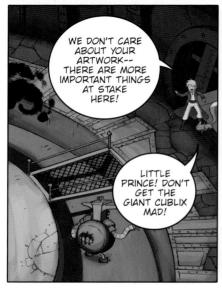

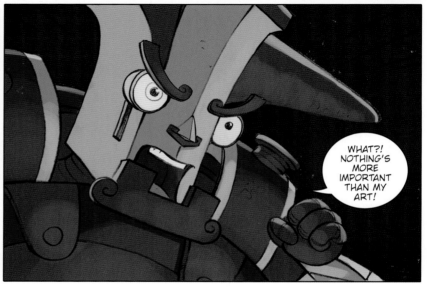

HEY!
WHERE'S
ALUMNIX?

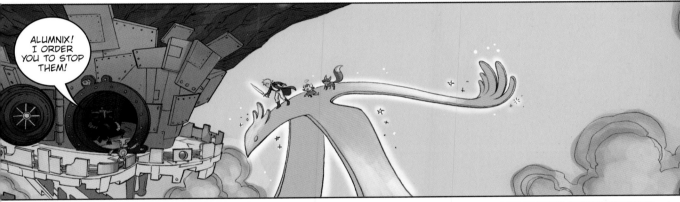

ALUMNIX!
I ORDER
YOU TO STOP
THEM!

YOU WON'T
ESCAPE SO
EASILY!

WHAT?!

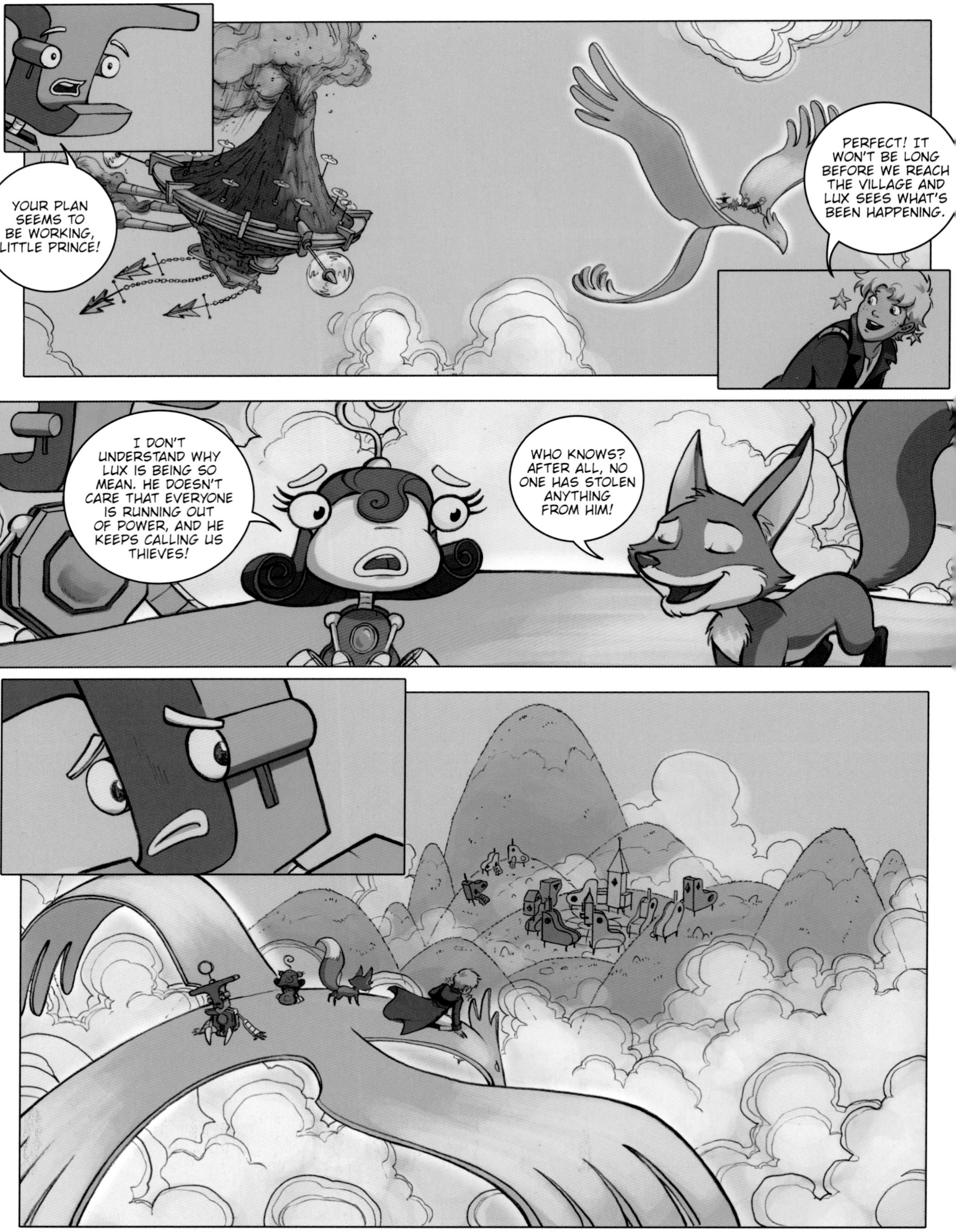
YOUR PLAN SEEMS TO BE WORKING, LITTLE PRINCE!
PERFECT! IT WON'T BE LONG BEFORE WE REACH THE VILLAGE AND LUX SEES WHAT'S BEEN HAPPENING.
I DON'T UNDERSTAND WHY LUX IS BEING SO MEAN. HE DOESN'T CARE THAT EVERYONE IS RUNNING OUT OF POWER, AND HE KEEPS CALLING US THIEVES!
WHO KNOWS? AFTER ALL, NO ONE HAS STOLEN ANYTHING FROM HIM!

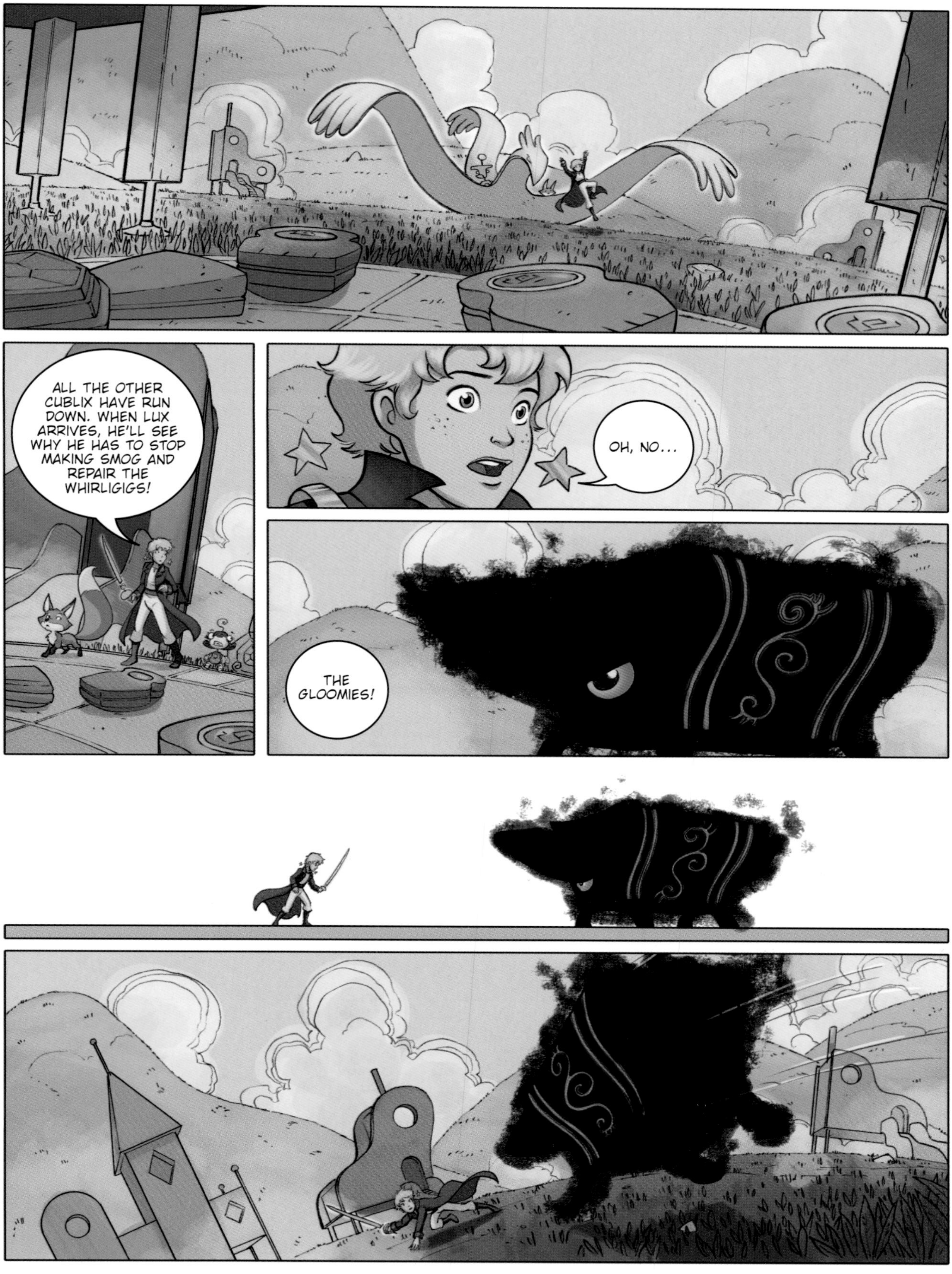
ALL THE OTHER CUBLIX HAVE RUN DOWN. WHEN LUX ARRIVES, HE'LL SEE WHY HE HAS TO STOP MAKING SMOG AND REPAIR THE WHIRLIGIGS!
OH, NO...
THE GLOOMIES!

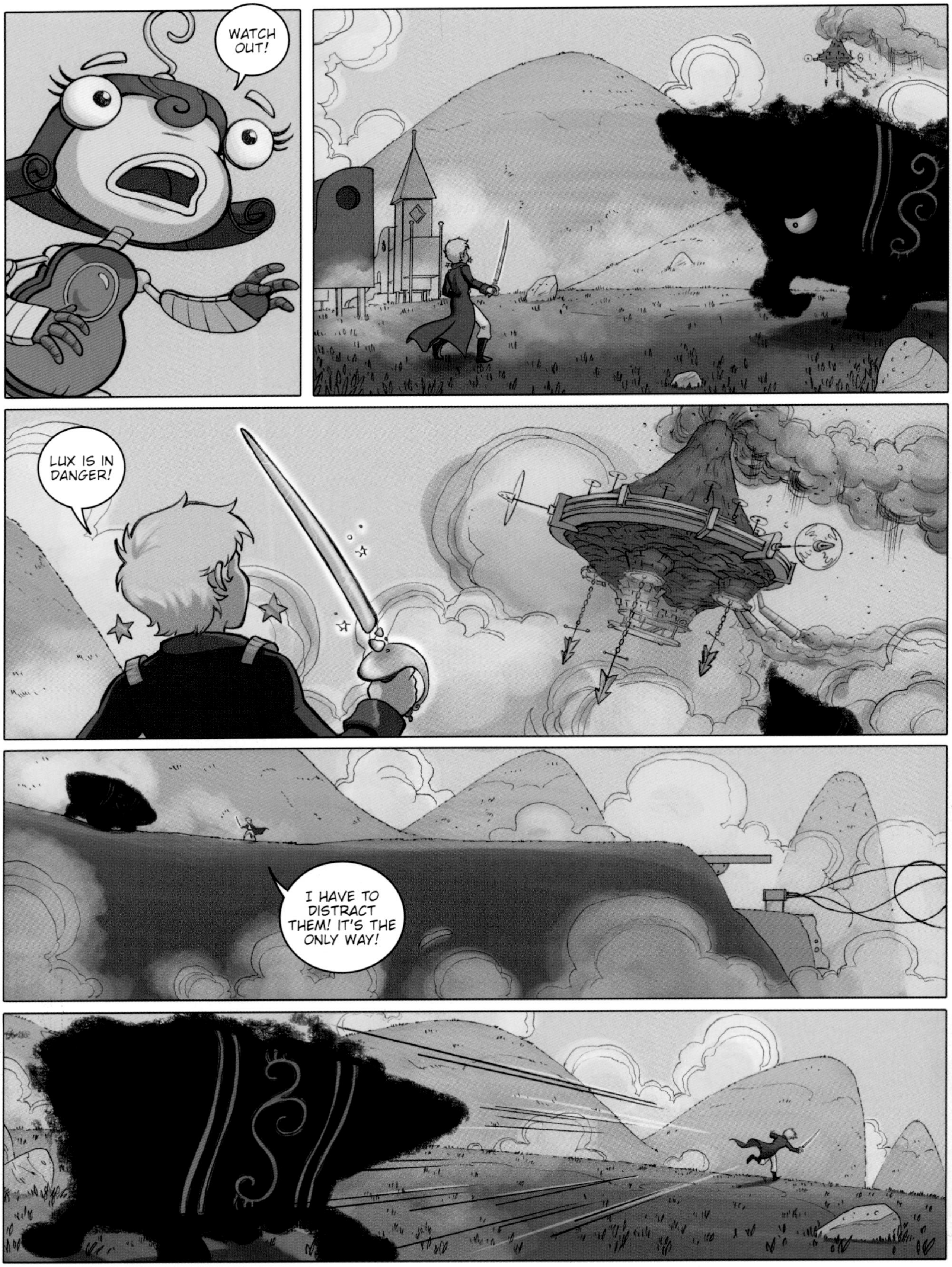
WATCH OUT!
LUX IS IN DANGER!
I HAVE TO DISTRACT THEM! IT'S THE ONLY WAY!

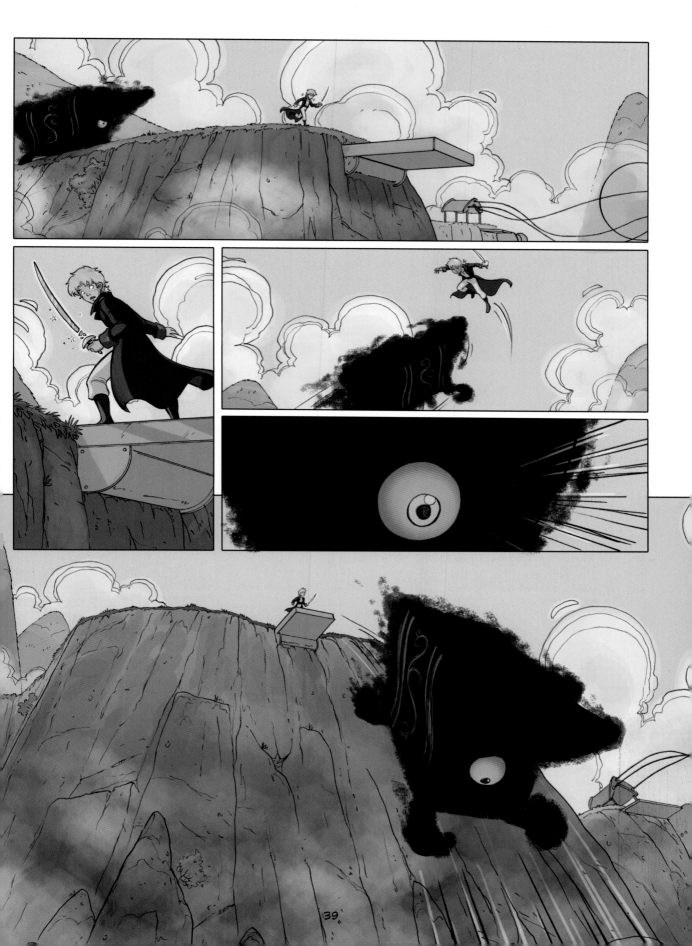

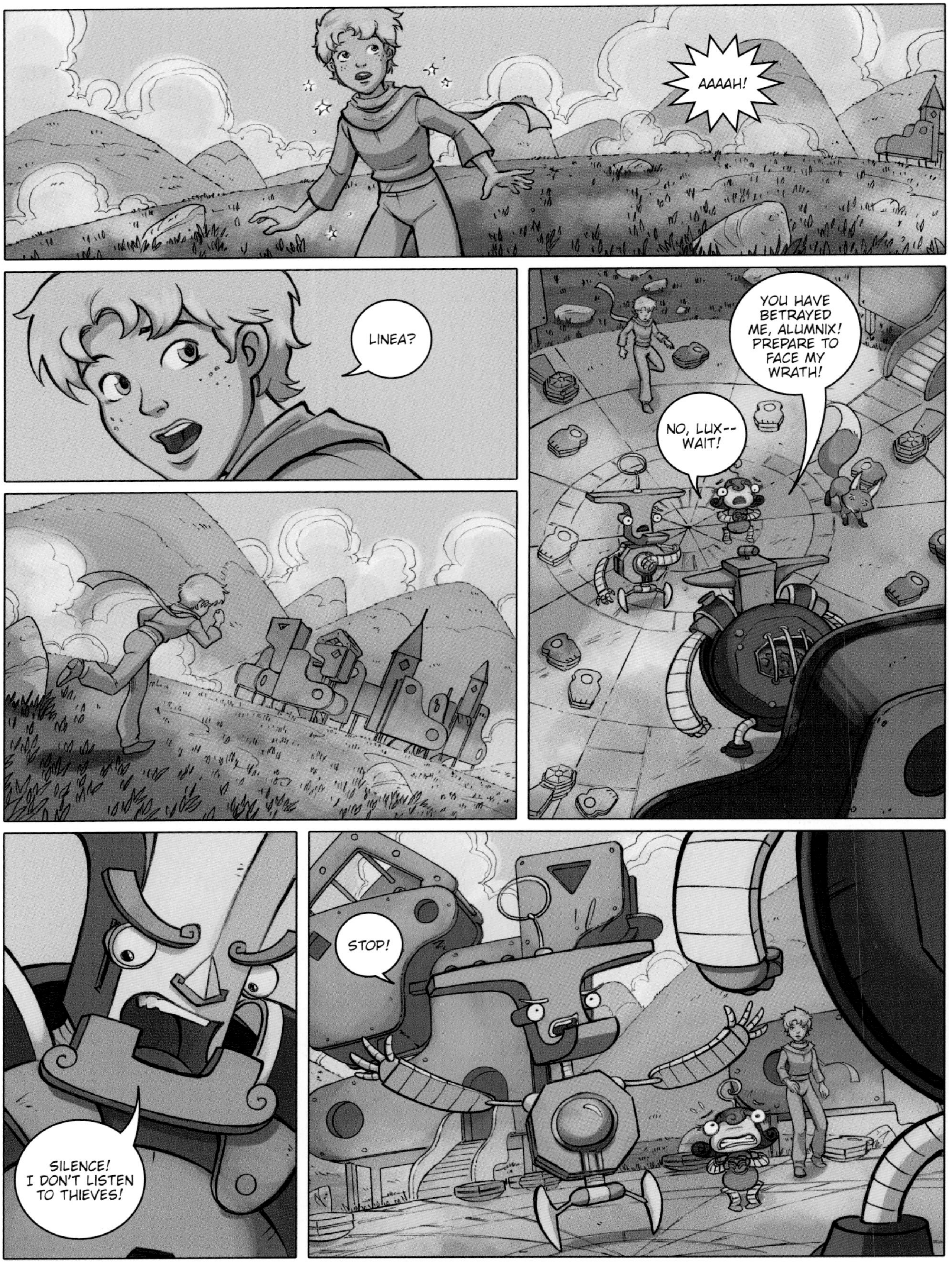

AAAAH!
LINEA?
YOU HAVE BETRAYED ME, ALUMNIX! PREPARE TO FACE MY WRATH!
NO, LUX-- WAIT!
SILENCE! I DON'T LISTEN TO THIEVES!
STOP!

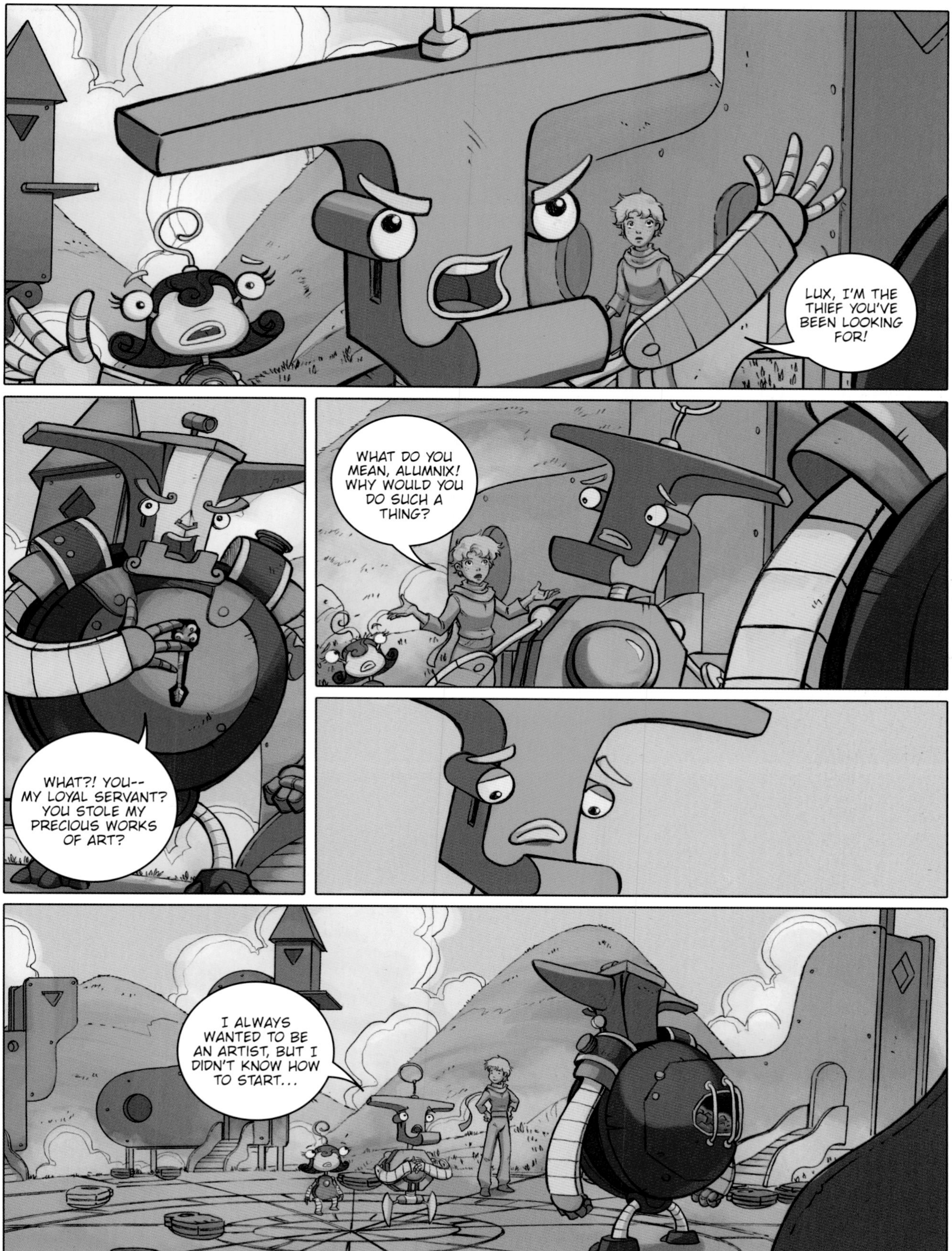
LUX, I'M THE THIEF YOU'VE BEEN LOOKING FOR!
WHAT?! YOU-- MY LOYAL SERVANT? YOU STOLE MY PRECIOUS WORKS OF ART?
WHAT DO YOU MEAN, ALUMNIX! WHY WOULD YOU DO SUCH A THING?
I ALWAYS WANTED TO BE AN ARTIST, BUT I DIDN'T KNOW HOW TO START...

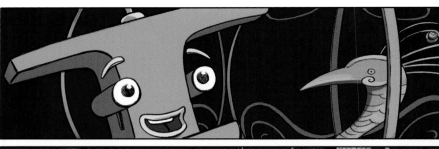
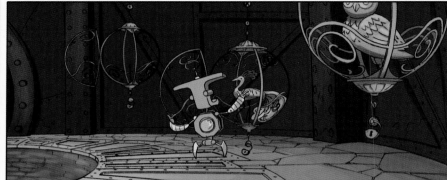

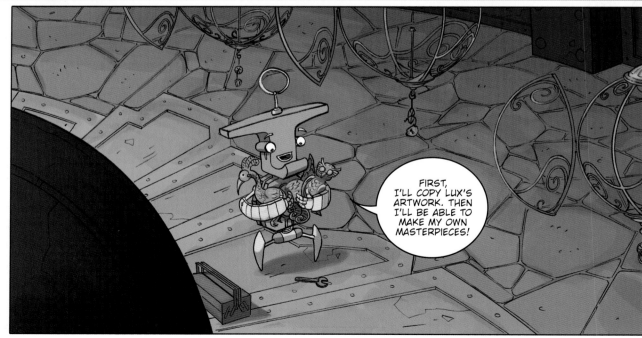

FIRST, I'LL COPY LUX'S ARTWORK. THEN I'LL BE ABLE TO MAKE MY OWN MASTERPIECES!

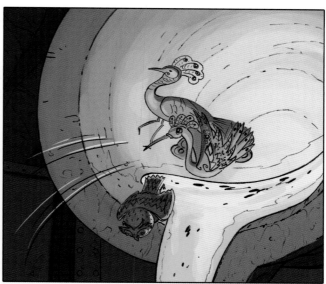

PING!

OH NO!
HE'LL NEVER
FORGIVE ME!

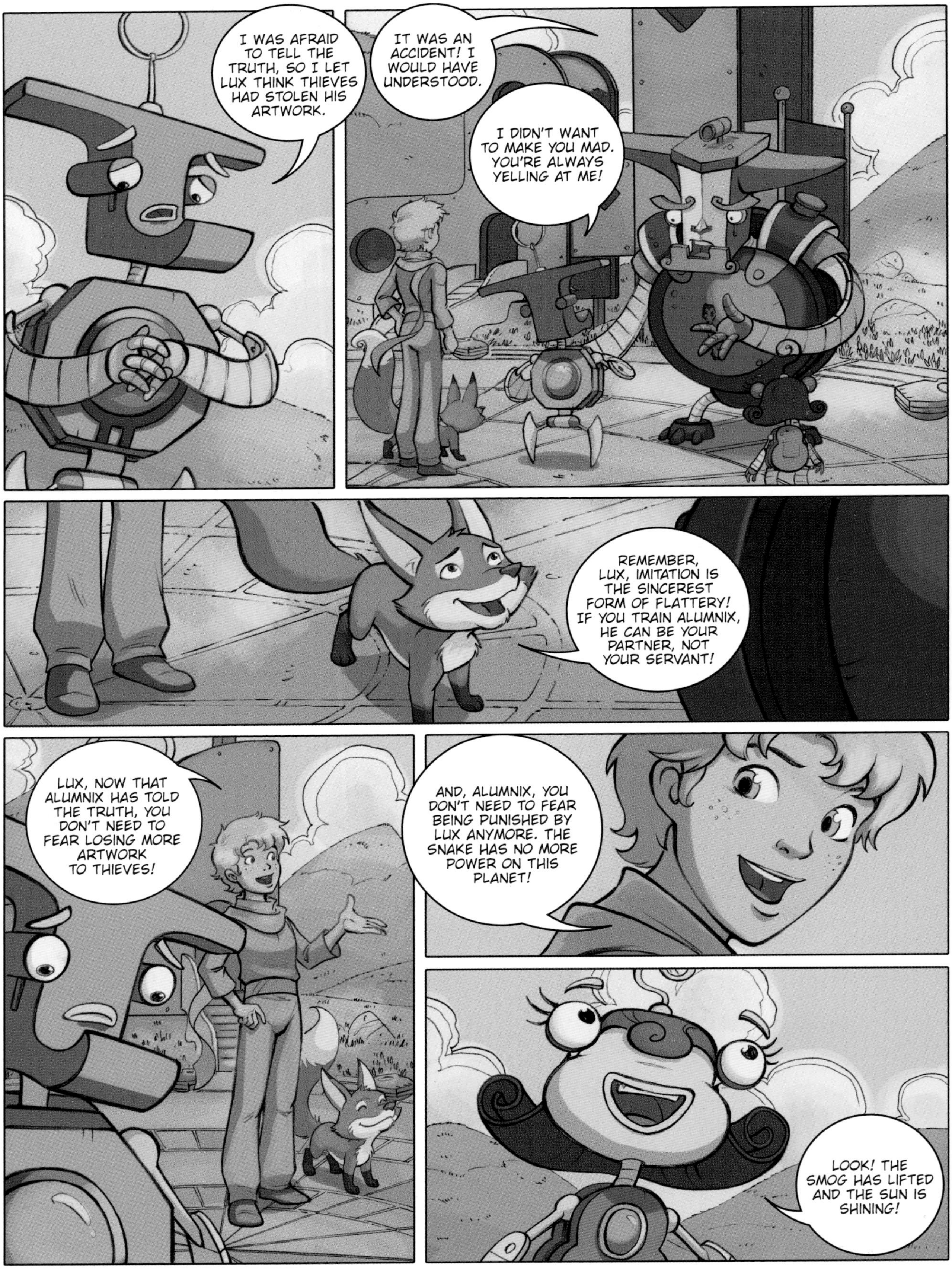
I WAS AFRAID TO TELL THE TRUTH, SO I LET LUX THINK THIEVES HAD STOLEN HIS ARTWORK.
IT WAS AN ACCIDENT! I WOULD HAVE UNDERSTOOD.
I DIDN'T WANT TO MAKE YOU MAD. YOU'RE ALWAYS YELLING AT ME!
REMEMBER, LUX, IMITATION IS THE SINCEREST FORM OF FLATTERY! IF YOU TRAIN ALUMNIX, HE CAN BE YOUR PARTNER, NOT YOUR SERVANT!
LUX, NOW THAT ALUMNIX HAS TOLD THE TRUTH, YOU DON'T NEED TO FEAR LOSING MORE ARTWORK TO THIEVES!
AND, ALUMNIX, YOU DON'T NEED TO FEAR BEING PUNISHED BY LUX ANYMORE. THE SNAKE HAS NO MORE POWER ON THIS PLANET!
LOOK! THE SMOG HAS LIFTED AND THE SUN IS SHINING!

BUT IT'S TOO LATE-- THEY'VE ALL RUN DOWN!

HOW CAN I RECHARGE THEM ALL? IT'S TOO GREAT A TASK!

I HAVE JUST THE SOLUTION!

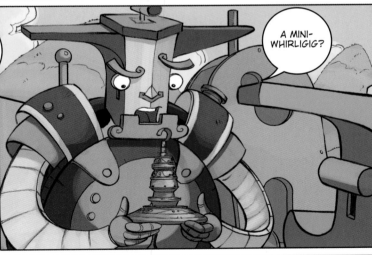

A MINI-WHIRLIGIG?

TRUST ME!

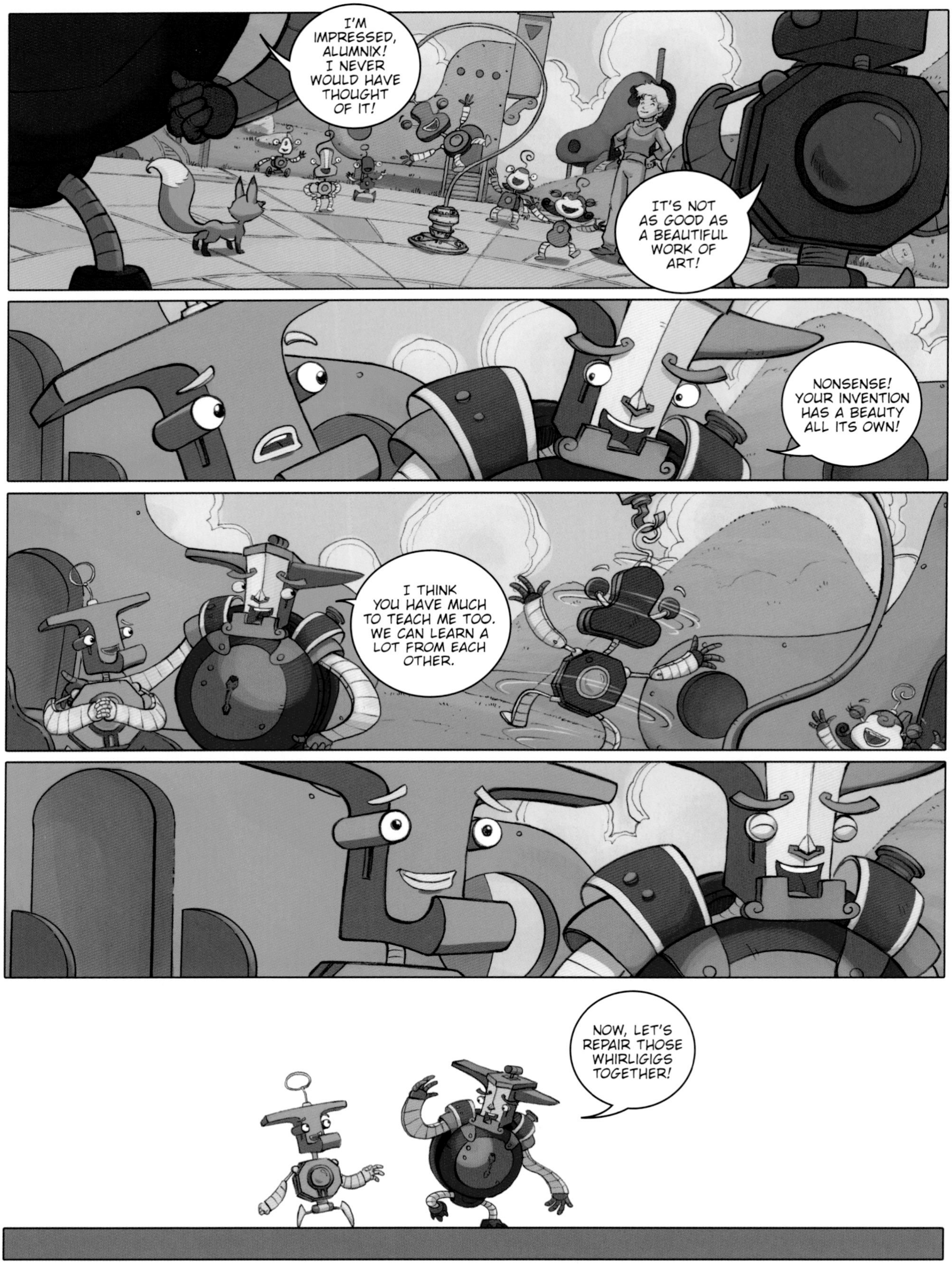
I'M IMPRESSED, ALUMNIX! I NEVER WOULD HAVE THOUGHT OF IT!
IT'S NOT AS GOOD AS A BEAUTIFUL WORK OF ART!
NONSENSE! YOUR INVENTION HAS A BEAUTY ALL ITS OWN!
I THINK YOU HAVE MUCH TO TEACH ME TOO. WE CAN LEARN A LOT FROM EACH OTHER.
NOW, LET'S REPAIR THOSE WHIRLIGIGS TOGETHER!

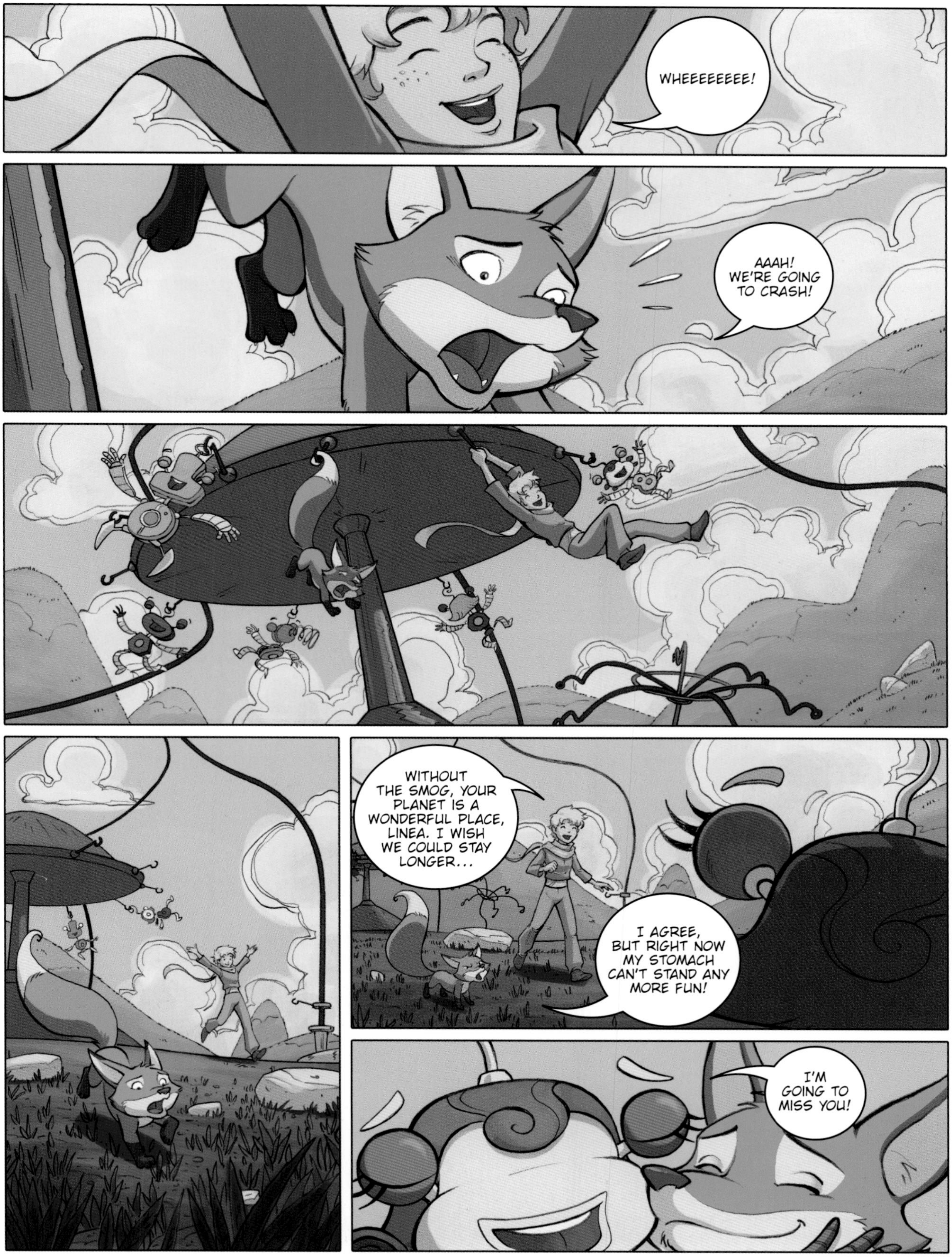
WHEEEEEEEE!
AAAH! WE'RE GOING TO CRASH!
WITHOUT THE SMOG, YOUR PLANET IS A WONDERFUL PLACE, LINEA. I WISH WE COULD STAY LONGER...
I AGREE, BUT RIGHT NOW MY STOMACH CAN'T STAND ANY MORE FUN!
I'M GOING TO MISS YOU!

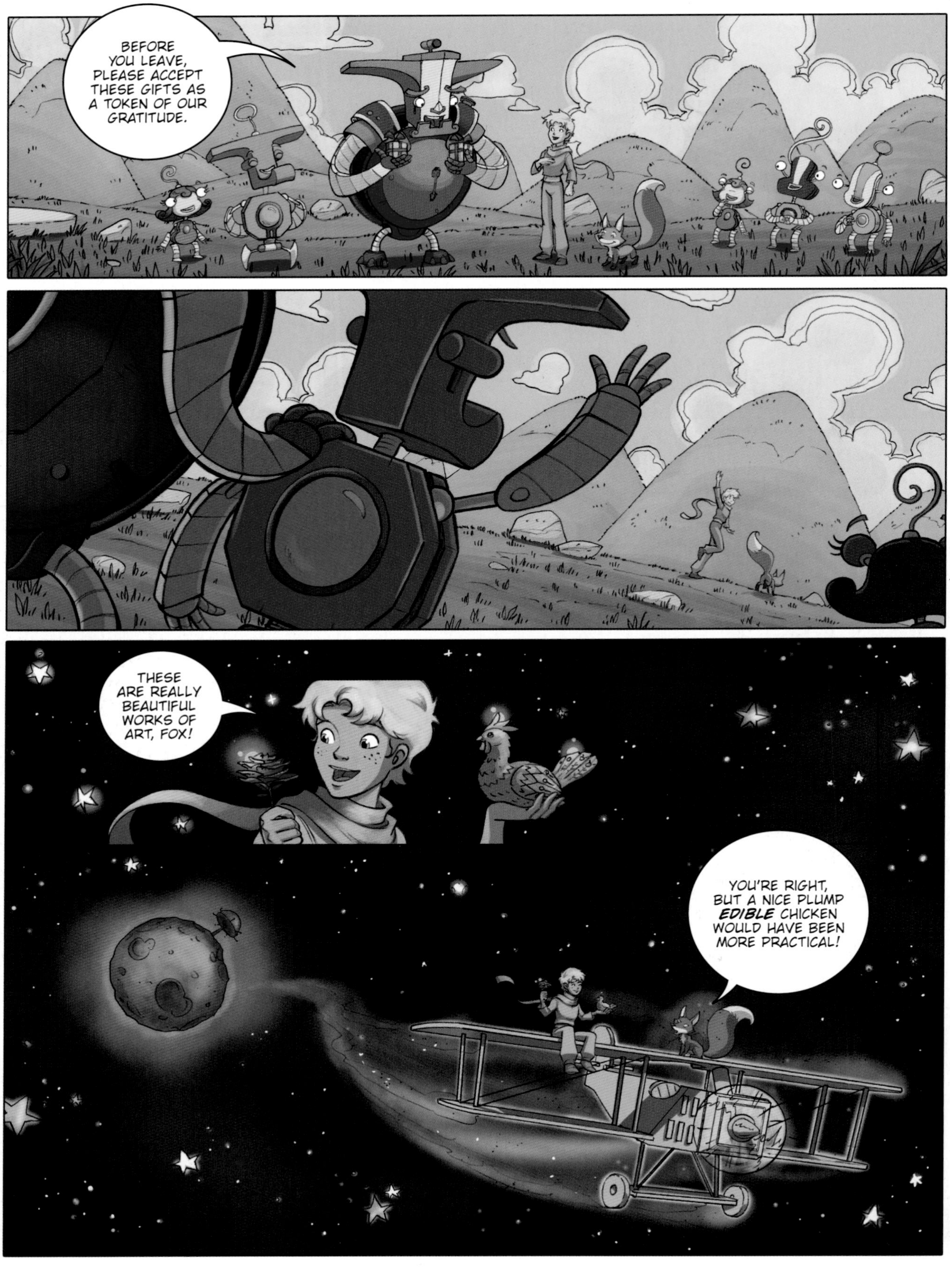
BEFORE YOU LEAVE, PLEASE ACCEPT THESE GIFTS AS A TOKEN OF OUR GRATITUDE.
THESE ARE REALLY BEAUTIFUL WORKS OF ART, FOX!
YOU'RE RIGHT, BUT A NICE PLUMP *EDIBLE* CHICKEN WOULD HAVE BEEN MORE PRACTICAL!

Read all the Books in *The Little Prince* series

Book 1: The Planet of Wind

Book 2: The Planet of the Firebird

Book 3: The Planet of Music

Book 4: The Planet of Jade

Book 5: The Star Snatcher's Planet

Book 6: The Planet of the Night Globes

Book 7: The Planet of the Overhearers

Book 8: The Planet of the Tortoise Driver

Book 9: The Planet of the Giant

Book 10: The Planet of Trainiacs

Book 11: The Planet of Libris

Book 12: The Planet of Ludokaa

Book 13: The Planet of Tear-Eaters

Book 14: The Planet of the Grand Buffoon

Book 15: The Planet of the Gargand

Book 16: The Planet of Gehom

Book 17: The Planet of the Bubble Gob

Book 18: The Planet of Time

Book 19: The Planet of the Cublix

Book 20: The Planet of Coppelius

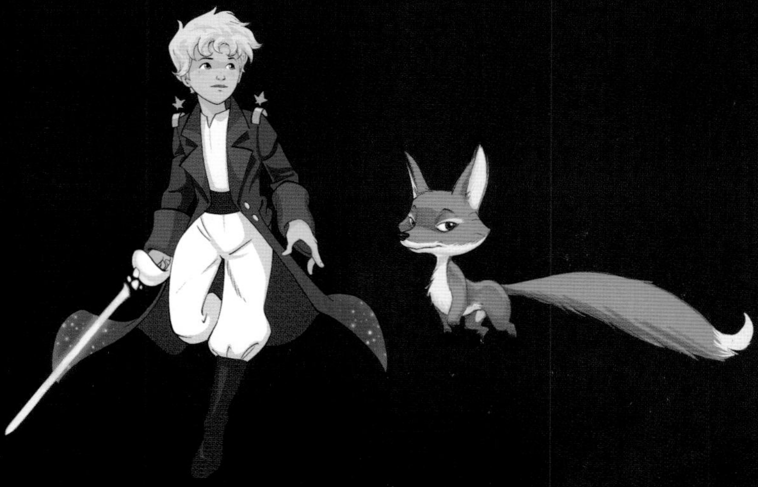

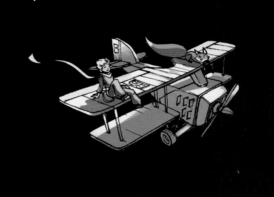

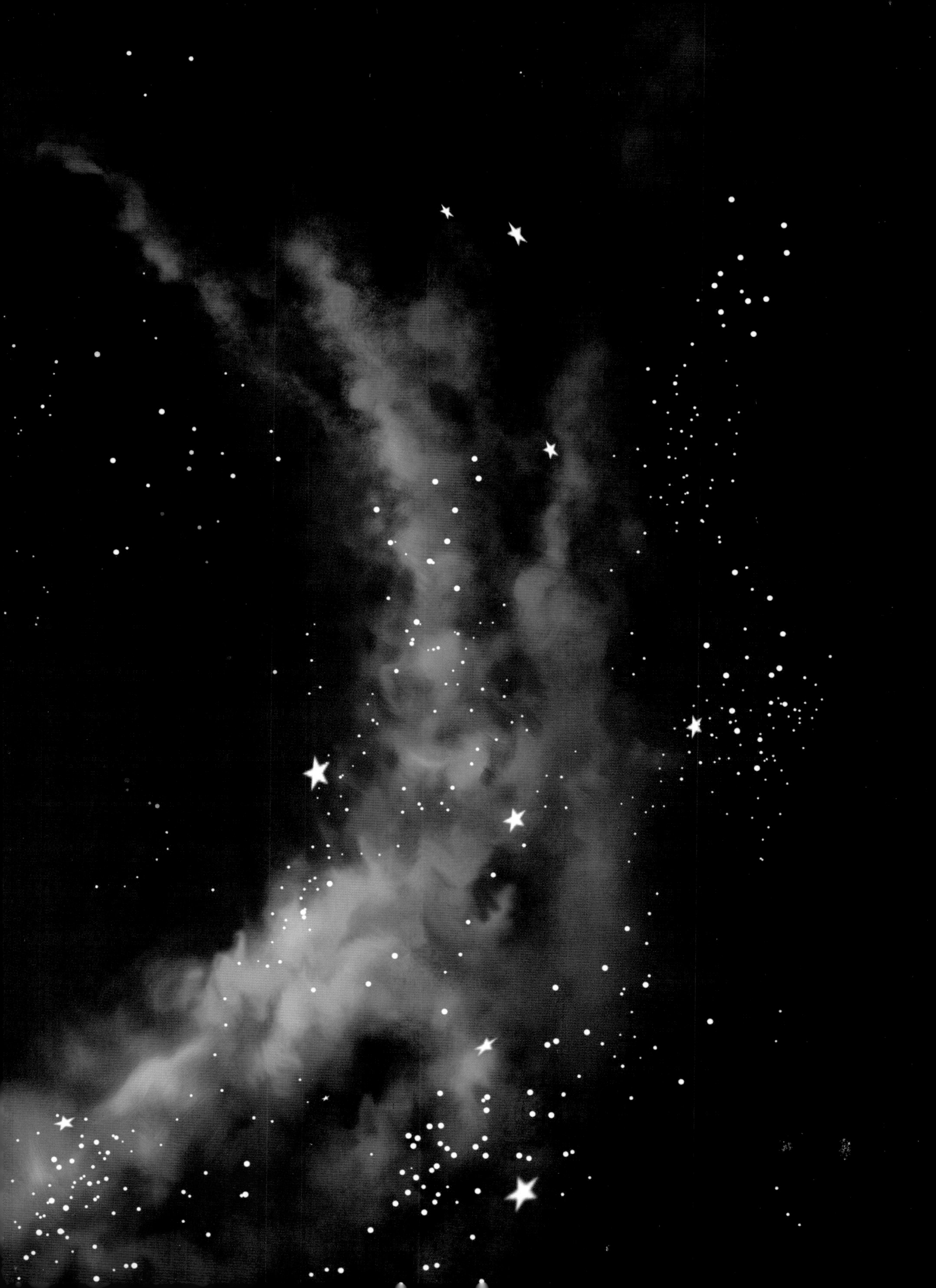